NOAH

7 BRIDES FOR 7 SOLDIERS
BOOK 6

New York Times Bestselling Author
CRISTIN HARBER

PROLOGUE

February, Washington, DC

THE SUN CRACKED through the open slats of Noah Coleman's blinds in the bedroom of his sparsely furnished Eastern market apartment. His Navy SEAL team had landed in Baltimore a little after one o'clock in the morning, and with the time change and travel, coupled with the exhaustion of the intense job, he crashed face-first into his pillow.

But it wasn't the sun keeping him awake. His roommate, FBI Special Agent Kenneth Murphy, banged on the wall. "Kenny, go away."

The noise didn't stop. Maybe Kenny was banging *again*, from what Noah's foggy and exhausted mind could tell.

"Stop," Noah muttered and turned over with his pillow, burying himself under the cool sheets. Two days without sleeping—Kenny could give him the morning.

"I hate to do this to you" came through the wall. "But you have to wake up."

Noah rolled onto his back again. He'd gone longer with less sleep. Kenny wouldn't bother him if it weren't important. "Hang on."

He pulled on a pair of sweatpants and grabbed his personal cell phone that had been on its charger since he'd left for the special forces op days ago. The screen awakened as he lumbered out of bed.

Twenty-seven notifications.

More than two notifications were unusual, and a dull sense of dread rolled through Noah as he opened his bedroom door and paced down the hallway, glancing at who had reached out. His folks. Lainey. And now Kenny who had banged on his wall when—Noah glanced at the time—his roommate should have been at work, and now faced him in their apartment. "What's wrong with my family?"

Kenny's clean-shaven face didn't have the answers. "All I know is your father called me."

Noah looked back at his notifications then scrolled through the text messages, finding generic but strongly worded "call as soon as you get this" requests.

Dad might've called Kenny, but it was Noah's cousin Lainey who would tell Noah the unfiltered truth.

He pulled up her name and pressed Send, holding the ringing phone to his ear. "Voicemail." He did the time-difference math and figured Lainey was either dropping her daughter off at preschool or walking into work.

"Really?" Kenny asked. "Your dad tracked me down at work then didn't pick up the phone?"

"I called my cousin first. She'll tell me what my parents will skirt around." With that many messages, texts, and a call to Kenny, his family back in Eagle's Ridge was competing to get to him first—or they wanted to make sure they heard from him between special ops. Either way, that type of call was easier when it wasn't sugarcoated. "I'll make a cup of coffee and try Lainey again. If she doesn't answer after that, then I'll call my dad."

Kenny nodded as he tossed his keys into the air. "I'm headed back in. If you need anything, let me know."

A cup of coffee later, Noah decided to call Lainey at work

instead of on her cell phone.

"Eagle's Ridge Pediatrics," the receptionist answered from the Coleman Center. "Can I help you?"

"Is Lainey Force in?"

"She is, but she's with a patient. If you have a question, I can send you to the nurse's voicemail and someone will get back to you—"

"This is Noah Coleman. I'll hold."

"Oh," the receptionist said, in a way that put him on alert. The hairs at the back of his neck stood on end as she hurried off the phone, and a recording of child health safety tips began to play. By the time he heard the first tip twice, his patience was running low.

"You're home." Lainey's sweet voice interrupted a useless-to-him tip about testing bathwater before putting a baby in it. Heaven help the woman who he had children with. Except, never mind. A family wasn't in his future. He was a SEAL, through and through. The military was his life. Not that he was wild or didn't want to settle down, but he wasn't the type to leave the service.

"What's wrong?"

"Noah, I'm so sorry."

Her voice stopped him cold, and tension pulsed at his temples. "For what? What the hell is going on in Eagle's Ridge?"

"You didn't talk to your dad?"

"No, dammit. I called you first. I *always* call you first."

"I'm sick, Noah," she whispered.

Exasperated, his forehead furrowed. "So, you get sick. You're a nurse. You're around kids all the time. They're little germ magnets. You're bound to get—"

"No, I really am, and I should have known better. Because

I *am* a nurse. Because I ignored signs and symptoms—"

"Lainey, stop." The tension in his temples froze, and his tired muscles stiffened. "What are you talking about?"

"I have cancer, Noah. Late-stage cancer."

A knot formed in his throat. Breathing through the pain seemed harder to survive than his op covert op in Serbia just forty-eight hours ago under the worst of circumstances. That job had been nearly mission impossible but deemed critical. He'd attacked the problem and won. "You fight it. Right? There's medicines, right? Like chemo and radiation. Surgery." He didn't even know what kind of cancer, but it sounded as though she'd already given up. "This isn't a death sentence."

"There are a lot of things I wish I had done differently. But more than anything, I need to talk to you about Bella. Can you come home? I can't do this over the phone, and not at work."

He pinched the bridge of his nose as his eyes seared, and he rolled his lips together. Lainey was his cousin, but they had been raised as though they were twins. His dad and her mom were fraternal twins, and Lainey and Noah were born so close together that with a family this close-knit, she seemed more like his sister than his cousin.

"I'm not coming home to plan your death and how to help Bella."

Lainey sniffled. "Of course you are, Noah. You're a Navy SEAL. You're my protector. This is who you are."

CHAPTER ONE

October
Eagle's Ridge, Washington State

NOAH HIT THE ground running that morning. As soon as he landed at Eagle's Ridge Airport, he had a list of action items to complete within certain time frames.

First, he swung by his parents' house for all the necessary hugs and catching up, promising his Aunt Virginia, Bella's grandma, that the last of her bags would be stowed safely in her own home by lunchtime. Noah checked that off his list before eleven in the morning.

He hit the grocery store, moving down the aisle as though he was on orders, grabbing essentials, even though Aunt Virginia had said she'd left plenty in the fridge and cupboards for him to cook. Noah was taking no chances. He had a plan, and that revolved around preparing recipes that were fast, reliable, and things he knew how to cook. As much as his aunt loved baked cinnamon apples as a side dish with dinner, if she left apples, they would eat them as apples were normally eaten—by biting into them.

Now, everything had been checked off his list—homecoming with minimal fanfare, groceries purchased and put up where he thought they should go, and a quick pit stop at Westbrook Real Estate to pick up the keys to Nuts and Bolts Auto Garage.

He was home an hour earlier than he'd expected. That was a good thing since Zane and Adam, the twins from high school, had stopped in to catch up since the last time he was in town. Noah needed the distraction. The closer his watch ticked to the time Bella would arrive home on the school bus, the more anxious he became.

The guys caught him up on friends they had in common, and Noah gave them a tour of Lainey's house. They all stared into Bella's glittery pink bedroom as if it might sprout the same ghost and goblin heads that were starting to pop up throughout Eagle's Ridge, announcing the start of the Halloween season.

"Dude, are you sweating?" Zane chuckled as he leaned against a wall decorated with vinyl star stickers.

"Of course he's sweating," Adam cracked. "What does he know about raising a kid?"

"Enough." But the tension knot at the back of his neck called BS.

Zane walked to a bookshelf, picked up a reading primer, and held up the cover, which showed a giraffe wearing ballet shoes. "Noah looks like he's been thrown into a war zone without training."

"I *haven't* had training," Noah mumbled. Nor could he explain why a giraffe would wear any shoes, much less pointy-toed ones.

Dancing wildlife wasn't his concern, though. Not when he hadn't had enough time to wrap his head around life changers like Lainey's death, departing the military, and starting a civilian life. It wasn't just parenting that he had to adjust to. His brilliant decision to buy Nuts and Bolts had seemed smart. What a great idea, being his own boss. Plus, Eagle's Ridge had missed the friendly, quirky auto shop.

But now he'd added "running a business" to the list of things he had no clue how to do, and he was researching how-tos like a madman. His search history continually jumped among related topics. In between Googling how to be a successful small business owner and how to raise a gifted, orphaned five-year-old, Noah had nearly short-circuited his brain. "I missed this day at SERE school."

Survival. Evasion. Resistance. Escape. The truth was, Noah didn't want to do the last three, and he would do a lot better than just surviving, but his start would no doubt be rocky.

"There's an upside." Zane chuckled. "At least you don't have to change diapers."

Adam raised his eyebrows as if in agreement. "What's your plan?"

"We know you have one," Zane said.

His plan? It was a work in progress and had been patch-worked together from all over the world. Noah liked the minutia of solving problems and how to fix them—or wire them, which was one of the reasons he was highly successful in the field of explosives. It wasn't all light a fuse and kaboom. He was known for his precise measurements after studying the circumstances, often under intense pressure, but also for *MacGyvering it*, and whatever was on hand for any purpose, in any condition, from diversion to survival.

Maybe that was why his plan was based on more than internet research. Family and friends gave him polite advice but mostly reassurances that he would do a great job parenting. Reassurance wasn't what he was looking for. Noah needed actionable intelligence, and he found the ones most likely to give their raw opinions and specific action items were the self-proclaimed mommy bloggers.

The websites were a treasure trove of information—from

ways to discipline children who swiped before they knew how to wipe to raising a gifted child in the era of information overload. And he had no time when sites contradicted one another. He simply picked the option that had the most agreeable comments then proceeded to outline his own crash course in Parenting 101.

While the best how-to advice came from the mommy bloggers, the most thought-provoking advice came unexpectedly during a special project deployments. Kunar, in particular. Their team allies, led by female tribal leaders in the mostly rural province, saw the worry and pain in his eyes when he couldn't sleep.

One tribal leader had explained to Noah that the day didn't start and end with the sun. Except common sense told him it did, as did the twenty-four hours on the clock.

It took him two days and one of his teammates calling home to ask his wife before Noah understood the concept of starting the day over. His teammate's wife explained that their kids would push an imaginary reset button for a fresh start to the day if their behavior needed a reboot.

Another tribal leader had taken Noah's hand. Hers was cold and leatherlike, her fingernails thick and short. But her grip had been powerful when she advised Noah that he should always say, "Tell me more."

She didn't let go until he held her eyes and promised he'd never let a child end a story without offering those three words. "Don't forget to listen" were her parting words when his SEAL team left Kunar. Only he knew what she meant.

But their advice wasn't a strategy, more like broad-spectrum tactics, and for now, he would take one day at a time, just as recommended by every expert, blogger, and advice-giver on childhood bereavement and kindergarten success.

"You do have a plan, right?" Zane's words pulled Noah back to the present. Zane gave Adam a side-eye as he inspected the row of glitter nail polish bottles as though they were live exhibits at the zoo.

"You know"—Noah backed them out of Bella's room—"there's a woefully inadequate amount of advice out there from the male and military perspective."

"There's a lot of bling in Bella's room." Adam lifted a bottle of gold polish. "Do you know what to do with that?"

Noah swatted it from his hand. "More than you do."

"Doesn't sound convincing," Adam teased. "I can't believe Noah doesn't have a plan. What's the world coming to? Glitter nail polish and Noah's planless—"

"I have a plan." But not one as detailed and long-range as Noah would've liked. "I figure tonight, we'll order pizza."

"Pizza's the big plan?" Adam led the way down the hall.

"Sure, why not?" Noah lifted his shoulder. "It's not like Bella needs a celebratory dinner for my return. Or her... *situation*. I just haven't been around as much as I would like to have been."

"*Situation*. Good word." Zane rolled his eyes.

Noah ignored him.

"Ryder called on the way here." Zane dropped onto the couch in the living room, and Adam sat next to him.

Noah leaned against the wall. "Ryder? How's he doing?"

"Good." Zane stretched back. "Actually, great."

"Good."

"He and Bailey are together."

Noah smiled at news of the twins' sister, laughing. "That's great. One big happy family."

Adam chuckled also. "She's sending over a casserole tonight."

"She is?" Noah cocked his eyebrow.

"We guessed you'd do pizza too, and she said nope, that Bella should have a home-cooked meal tonight."

"What's wrong with pizza?" Noah hadn't thought about food other than to know they'd be hungry, and pizza sounded easy and good.

Bailey had known he'd do pizza and that he *shouldn't*. Noah didn't even know why pizza was the wrong choice, yet his intuition would be screaming if an enemy was nearby.

"No idea," Adam said. "All she said was *nope*."

"Nope? Huh." Maybe he should revisit the idea of granola bars and the chocolate instant breakfast drink he'd picked out at the store, though he had made an effort to look at the label. The two items checked all the boxes that seemed important— protein, carbs, calcium, and vitamins. Nutrient-packed. "What do you think about instant shakes and power bars for breakfast?"

They both shrugged, and Adam said, "Yeah, works for me. But don't kids eat things like Cheerios and milk?"

"Think about it, man." Zane wrinkled his nose. "All those bars and shakes make your SEAL team fart like you hit up Beanee Weenee night at the All You Can Eat. What do you think that's going to do to a kid?"

Noah scrunched his nose, semi-missing the nausea-inducing rankness. "Yeah, I can see that being a problem."

Adam chuckled. "I'll text Bailey. Maybe she can throw in a box of Cheerios on the casserole run."

"Appreciate it." Noah checked his watch. "Wow, they're almost here."

"Who else?"

He shook his watch back into place. "Do you know Teagan Shaw?"

"I do," Zane said. "She knows Harper, the new librarian."

Adam waggled his eyebrows, letting it be known there was more to the story. "His new girlfriend."

Zane's proud face lit up. "That too. Not so new, though."

Noah stretched, trying to shake his unease from his muscles. "A lot has changed since our days in detention, staring at the good-looking teacher."

Adam nodded.

"Miss Woody." Zane said her name reverently, and Noah repeated it, though that wasn't really her name. Woods was.

Still, the thought of the woman made him dopey, as if they were fifteen years old again. They had her so high on a pedestal, Noah was surprised they hadn't broken their necks trying to flirt. "Our high school game must have been…" He made a face. "Underwhelming."

"Yup," Zane deadpanned.

"Ha. I don't know about you, but my game was on point." Adam tugged on the collar of his shirt, smirking like they were again teenagers who thought they were hot stuff.

Zane knocked his twin's hand down. "On point like a Q-tip."

Adam laughed. "What does that even mean?"

Noah ignored the antics of the boys, who were acting as if they were roaming the school halls again. "What's she doing these days?"

"High school principal," Zane explained.

"*Really?*" Noah's jaw went slack as Adam and Zane sobered, and they shared a moment of silence over what had to be every teenage boy's biggest dilemma—not wanting to be called to the principal's office but *wanting* to be called to the principal's office.

"Yeah. Those were the days. When Adam didn't have a

chance with Miss Woody, and—"

"Like I was the only one who tried for her attention," Adam interrupted. "Remember when you connected me with your FBI contact?"

"My roommate? Kenny?" Noah asked.

"That's the guy."

"Of course, I remember." Noah nodded.

"Long story short, he helped me sort through a few issues, and now I'm with the woman I plan to spend the rest of my life with. I wouldn't care if Miss Woody walked in the door now or not."

Noah stared at them, realizing that not only had he moved back to Eagle's Ridge but also that everyone he knew there seemed to have settled down. Not that he'd be dating. What did it even matter? Now he had a kid. "A lot's changed."

"Not that much." Zane smacked Adam with a pillow from the couch. "If Miss Woody walked in, all of us would do a double take."

They burst out laughing. Adam threw his hands up. "Hey, hey. Lay off."

Noah checked the time again. "Teagan and the school bus will be here soon."

Adam pushed off the couch and clapped his hands. "Guess we'll roll."

Zane stood as well. "Teagan's smart and knows everyone."

Those were his mother's exact words when describing Teagan, and she'd also noted that Teagan's son was close to Bella. Besides his mother and Aunt Virginia, it seemed Teagan was the other person who'd helped the most with Bella before he could come home.

Noah slapped his buddy on the back. "Thanks, man."

They walked toward the front of Lainey's house. "For what

it's worth, I'd have fed the kid pizza too." Adam kicked one of Noah's bags that remained by the front door. "Think it should look like you plan on staying?"

He ran his hand over his jaw and into his hair. "It feels weird to move into Lainey's bedroom."

"I'd figure it out fast. And if you don't, Bailey'll let you have it."

Noah chewed the inside of his mouth. "I haven't cleaned up the guest room."

Zane shook his head as he opened the front door. "No one says unpack this second, man. Just get it out of the hallway."

A Subaru pulled into the driveway, catching their attention.

"Tell Teagan we say hey. You know she's the school counselor, right?" Zane tacked on as they stepped down the front porch, cutting through the front yard and waving a friendly hello to Teagan.

No, he did not. He'd have to remember to ask his mom and aunt why they'd neglected to mention that the woman dropping by had caretaking credentials. Then again, that was one of the many things Noah had no clue about today. Pizza. Storing bags. Inviting school counselors over.

Noah stepped out, tossing an arm to wave bye then greet the woman he knew only as Teagan, the mother of Bella's friend. The guys pulled away as the Subaru's door opened.

"Teagan?" He strode forward, extending his hand to the confident woman whose brown hair picked up a hint of red in the sun. "Hey there. Noah Coleman."

"Nice to meet you." Her vibrant amber eyes weren't as warm as her smile, though they were beautiful, and her cool handshake firmly gripped his. "Teagan Shaw."

"Nice to meet you." Their hands parted, and he immediately wished he'd known the guidance-counselor aspect of Mrs. Shaw before inviting her over, whether Bella and her son were close or not. He had the immediate sense that he was undergoing an evaluation, which he would fail miserably. Hell, he'd only been stateside for less than forty-eight hours, and most of that time had been spent on travel and untangling his life from the United States Navy SEALs, something he thought he'd never do until he retired. "So."

She smiled crisply.

He tried for something a little less frigid. "You've known Bella for a while?"

"I have. Since she was very young."

Noah didn't know if that was a finished thought because he could've sworn she left off *And who are you? Where have you been?* Was it an immediate dislike for him, or didn't she trust him? Maybe the better question was, why should she trust him? Hell, why did he want her to?

He glanced away, ignoring that she wasn't hard on the eyes. Not that he would notice at a time like this. Was he even meant to be a parent?

Noah cleared his throat and acted as though she wasn't the first woman he'd seen before. "What's your kid's name?"

"Will."

"Sounds strong."

Her eyes narrowed. "How much do you know about Bella?"

"Right now?" Noah took a deep breath then gave an awkward grin. "Less than I'm going to know tonight."

From the looks of it, Teagan didn't find that as amusing as he did. "She's a good girl."

Well, no kidding. She was Lainey's daughter. Of course, Bella was a good girl. Noah would go out on a limb and say she was an amazing girl. Instead he rolled his lips together, and he and Teagan squared off awkwardly. His jaw was tight. Frustrated that this woman was so quick to judge, Noah tried to focus on his plan and the advice he'd been given, mostly because Teagan was only protecting his niece. "Tell me more."

A delicate, if not careful, smile curled on Teagan's lips. "About Bella?"

"Sure." He paused, surprised how well that had worked. "Or her and Will."

Teagan's dark brown hair lifted on a breeze, highlighting its red hue. "They're best friends. I can barely pull them apart."

"Best friends," Noah repeated.

Teagan finger combed her hair back in place as the wind tried to lift it again. "They believe in magic and wishes. They tell stories and dreams to each other."

"Like a little boyfriend-girlfriend?"

"No, I think they always pretend to be brother and sister."

"Gotcha."

"You've been told Bella's too young for our gifted program?"

"Yes."

"That's my background, and I keep an eye on her and those resources at school. So, if you need to bounce ideas, questions—anything, really—consider me available."

He nodded. "I appreciate that."

"It's also my job to make sure that her home and school life balance."

"Makes sense." Given that she was a guidance counselor, but what was Teagan getting at?

"I was the school's point of contact with your parents."

"I know. My mom is the one who set this up," he said, starting to feel defensive.

Teagan's eyes crinkled as she studied him. "Are you ready for this, Noah? She's been through so much."

"You think I don't know that?"

"And you're new back in town."

Again, the obvious. "What's your point?"

Teagan chewed on her bottom lip. "Your mom mentioned you were pulled out of a war zone recently. Like, last week."

He grit his molars. "Yeah, Mrs. Shaw, a week ago today, I was in Serbia. What about it?"

"Wait, hang on." She stepped closer. "You're hearing me all wrong."

"Maybe your delivery is lacking."

Her face pinched, and it hit him in the gut, though she'd been a bulldog moments ago.

"I can tell it was, and—" She inched back, staring toward the sky before turning back to him. "I don't know you, but Lainey was a good friend, and I love Bella. I'm sorry I came off as abrupt. I just can't stand to see her hurt again, and you're an unknown."

Noah's jaw relaxed. "I'm glad she has you in her corner."

Teagan gave a noncommittal smile.

"And I hope that you don't find me an unknown for long. I'm an open book. Family's my world. Always has been, even if you never heard of me before."

Her smile showed more teeth that time. "Heard of you, yes. Bella thinks you walk on water." The happiness faded. "Lainey did too."

Noah swallowed the unexpected burst of pain in his throat. "If we're being honest, I have a few tricks up my sleeve."

Teagan laughed, and thank God he did too. He didn't want to tear up in front of a woman he barely knew. But she had been on the forefront of a battle that he hadn't been able to wage in person.

Noah tipped his head back and looked at the sky, letting the cool northwest breeze blow over him. He smiled into the sun as it warmed his face for a moment, before he looked back at Teagan. "Thank you. From a Navy SEAL to a… soldier of, I don't know, social work. Thank you."

Her forehead scrunched. "You're welcome?"

He got a kick out of her. He glanced sideways at her smirk, and they cracked up. Letting loose, just knowing that he could hurt and still find amusement in life's everyday silliness, felt great.

"You've had the most honest reaction to my guardianship. Everyone is a cheerleader." Family and friends had promised that it would be all right, explaining that if anyone could persevere through a transition like this, he could.

"They mean well. I meant well."

He scrubbed a hand over his face. "People say that no one knows what they're doing, and that she's so smart, that whatever I screw up, she'll pick up the slack. But this?" He blew out, shaking his head. "This is next level."

A yellow school bus rounded the corner, and Noah's heart thundered in his chest as it had the first time he'd buckled in for a simulated helicopter crash into dark water. He knew he was strapped tight, that impact wouldn't be that bad, but the Navy had programmed their crash to gyrate and twist as rushing water filled the small space. He'd escape, he'd survive, but it might be hell on the way.

Teagan touched his arm, tapping him twice as his high school football coach had done. "If you need a helping hand, I'm handy."

The school bus came to a stop, and that was what he needed—not his friends, parents, or bloggers sharing advice and answering questions. He needed help. Why did it take until this moment for him to realize what he knew instinctively on the job? The most complicated tasks needed teamwork.

The yellow doors at the front of the bus angled open, and his pink-and-glitter niece descended the two stairs in one jump before landing on the sidewalk with a little boy protectively coming up behind her.

"Thanks," he said. "I could use the occasional teammate." Because it was game on as the biggest of life changers ran toward him with open arms.

CHAPTER TWO

TEAGAN'S FINGERS CURLED around the purse strap as if it was a lifeline. She'd known every person who had cared for the little girl while Lainey had been sick, and after she passed. Teagan and Noah had just had their tense moment. The day was chock-full of emotion and the unknown, and she couldn't be a tenth as uncertain as Noah was right now. Still, she worried whether Noah was the right man for the job.

"Uncle Noah!" Bella's bright eyes and exuberant smile showed no hesitation, despite the reason he was here, as she bound from the school bus and skipped, with Will warily remaining close. Like mother, like son. He too didn't want Bella's life to have any more hiccups.

Though it wasn't as if Virginia and Michael could continue to care for Bella. The Strams were older, and with Michael's hearing fading and their mobility slowing down, everyone had decided while Lainey was still healthy and active that Bella's grandparents shouldn't be the primary caretakers for the long term. They would keep Bella only while Lainey went to hospice and then until Noah could come home.

Will hung back and let his best friend go as Bella jumped into Noah's arms. The uncle-niece reunion was sweet, though Will didn't seem interested, and Teagan motioned for him to come closer as she walked toward her son, stopping just off the driveway, in the thick green grass where Bella and Noah had crouched. Teagan kissed the top of Will's head. "Hey, baby. How was your day?"

"Fine."

"What'd you do?" She wrapped her arm around his shoulder, embracing him, but he was as rigid as a white pine.

"Nothing."

The reply was typical for any kid, but today his voice floated away on the northwest breeze, more distracted than normal. When Will didn't return the hug, Teagan squeezed his side. It was time to put her profession to work at home. "Which color marker did you use the most today?"

"Blue," he mumbled. "I drew the sky. And then the rain. You couldn't see the rain until I pressed really hard to make the drops, and then Bella said the sky looked like it was crying."

"Was it crying?"

"Nope." He shook his head. "And she's a crying expert."

All of Teagan's heartstrings pulled simultaneously. "I know, baby. She's had a hard couple months. But that's why you're such a good friend."

The long middle-of-the-night calls with Lainey rushed back, from years ago when Lainey's husband Davis had died. Lainey had worried how it might screw up Bella when no one from his side of the family came to the funeral. She didn't want old Eagle's Ridge drama to taint Bella because her father had married into the *uppity* side of the river, abandoning his roots.

In Teagan's opinion, they had abandoned him and their blood, but at least they showed their true colors.

She shuddered. Would she rather have the unknown wild card of a Navy SEAL raising Bella or family members who wouldn't attend a funeral? Obviously, Noah, and it wasn't her call, anyway. Lainey had decided on him long ago, and Teagan agreed with her. But that didn't mean the decision was one hundred percent apprehension free.

"But." Will fidgeted. "Bella stopped crying when her mom stopped hurting."

She swallowed an emotional lump in her throat. "I know that too, baby."

At least, it had seemed that Bella was more at peace. Teagan and Will stared at the man on his knees in front of his niece. Noah wasn't what Teagan had pictured, and she'd never imagined he would be that handsome. Given Bella's family similarities, Teagan assumed he would have brown hair and eyes. What she didn't expect was how expressive he was without saying a word or how caring his questions were and how softly his voice carried when she knew he was a professional military man with determination and drive.

There was an all-knowing edge to his face, where sun lines creased the corners of his eyes and laugh lines surrounded his mouth. Noah had to be tired—and overwhelmed, not that that would be an excuse for Teagan to cut him too much slack—but he held himself tall, even when on his knees with Bella.

"Is he going to be a good friend?" Will asked.

"Grown-ups aren't always supposed to be a friend." She pulled Will around to face her so they weren't staring. Well, not staring as blatantly. Teagan still kept a close eye over Will's shoulder. "What did you eat first from your lunch box?"

"Yogurt raisins." He peeked around her shoulder. "Bella didn't eat much."

"I can appreciate that. Maybe she was nervous?"

"Think so. Her tummy feels funny too."

"That happens sometimes."

"Why are they so happy, then?" A thousand questions crossed his precious forehead as he tried to understand the intricacies of extended family.

Sometimes Teagan didn't even understand that concept. "Do you love Grandma Sue?"

A silly smile replaced the tight one. "Well, yeah."

"But do you know her very well?" Teagan tapped him on the nose. "You might be anxious to see her. When you do, you're very happy."

The dots connected in his mind, and his scowl softened as a little O formed on his lips. "Can I go over and say hi now?"

Teagan glanced over. Bella, all sunshine and smiles, was tugging Noah toward them until Will took off. It was quite the sight, the wisp of the girl and the thick, muscled man. Then Bella let go, and Noah remained in place and let his gaze follow the kids. His face was a mystery of triumph and terror.

Teagan bit her lip, watching the tough guy sweat the small stuff. He was in the deep end—so far that he couldn't find a proverbial purse strap to cling to if he'd wanted one.

Bella trotted over to Teagan's side, pushing onto her toes. "Can we go inside?"

She had just established the pecking order of who was in charge. Bella had asked Teagan—not Noah—if they could go inside the house Noah would now live in. Teagan lifted her eyebrows toward Noah. "I don't know. Can they?"

He sucked his cheeks in, as though he didn't know if they could go in and play or not. Maybe Noah had planned on making decisions only for Bella, and now he had to make or punt a choice for Will as well.

Teagan half twisted his way, deferring. "Because it's good with me if Will plays for a bit longer."

Picking up on her cue, Noah nodded, his square jaw loosening. "Sure. Have at it."

The kids took off through the front door like steamrollers, and she closed the small gap between the sturdy yet wildly unsteady man with less speed but even greater intention. "That wasn't a test of your command."

"I'm sorry?" The corner of his eyes crinkled as though he didn't like that she might've read his thoughts.

Smiling quietly, she shrugged. "Kids default to routine. I grant permission more often than you. It was more normal for Bella to ask my permission even though this is your house."

The tendons strained as he cracked his neck and popped his shoulders. "It's Lainey's."

"Well…" She ignored how he stretched his body and focused on how adults dealt with the stress of losing a loved one. Other than continuing education hours and occasional practicums, she'd never had to work with adults. Kids were different in how they alleviated stress.

Noah crossed his bicep over his chest and kneaded his muscle, then he repeated the same on the other side before shaking out his arms. Teagan decided the only thing she could focus on was the two-level stone-and-cedar home. That was safe and appropriate to gawk at. Lainey had always called it a cottage because of the fairy gardens she and Bella had planted in the backyard. "That was true. But it's your house now."

Noah quit his fidgeting and stared at the dark gray-blue paint and the round accent rocks as if he couldn't comprehend that he would lay his head to rest inside the charming little house filled with bedtime stories and fairy tales. "I don't know…"

"It is yours, Noah," Teagan urged.

"You don't know that."

True, she hadn't seen a will or any estate documents. She'd never asked or even thought to. But she did know that Lainey had arranged for Bella to be completely provided for, and part of that meant that the little girl had a trust to be administered by her guardian, funded by what came from life insurance. Even if the Forces weren't well off, the Strams were, and neither Lainey's parents nor the Colemans, Noah's side of the family, would let Bella struggle financially.

"I know enough," she countered. Lainey's house would likely be paid for from the trust, and that could give Noah wiggle room to get Nuts and Bolts running. Teagan had wondered why he didn't just find a job, but she knew now why he'd jumped headfirst into business ownership. Noah Coleman was such a Navy SEAL. Go after big things. Do them well.

"Sounds about right for Eagle's Ridge." He cast a sideways glance. "Everyone knows something."

They walked slowly toward the stone entryway as their easy conversation fell into an awkward silence. Was he suggesting she'd been gossiping? About him? It was time to change the subject. "I heard you're going to open Nuts and Bolts again."

Noah sighed and ran his hand through the back of his close-cut hair. "Yeah, yeah." He held the front door open for her, stepping back so Teagan could walk into the familiar house. "I think it's going to be a good thing."

The door clicked shut behind them, and he passed her, leading the way to the living room. She stepped over a couple of bags, wondering if he planned on sticking around for a while, then bit her tongue, wanting to trust Lainey's decision. "It will be. The town's already buzzing that it will open soon."

"Really?" he asked.

"It'd be great for everyone if you opened in time for Halloween."

His brow furrowed. "Why?"

"Oh, you don't remember," she said, sitting down on the love seat.

"Refresh my memory."

Teagan toyed with her hair, recalling year after year of holidays. "Let's see. There was a lot to choose from."

"You're stalling. Must not be that memorable." He winked.

"Picking the best of the best." She pulled her hair into a ponytail. "December was big for the holidays. But because the Halloween parade goes right by there, they went *big*. And they handed out candy in front of the parking lot."

"Oh, right!" He made a throwing motion. "I forgot about the Halloween parade."

The parade where the sidewalk watchers and storefront merchants threw candy and the kids in costumes walked down the street. An Eagle's Ridge tradition. "Well, I'm glad you remembered now."

Noah's eyebrows jumped as he readied to throw another imaginary handful of candy. "Yeah? Why's that?"

"Because the kindergarten crew take it *very* seriously, and you have some serious costume planning and decorating of Nuts and Bolts to figure out."

His face pinched as though he'd just realized that Bella would be walking in the parade too. "Awesome."

Well, darn it. Maybe her warning and amusement were off on their timing. "I can help with the costume. Easy, no problem."

"Nah, I've got it." He waved away her offer.

"You're going to need help sometimes," Teagan pointed out.

"On a Halloween costume?" He rolled his eyes. "I'll take Help for One Hundred on bigger issues, Alex."

Teagan winked. "Bella doesn't do typical costumes."

"That's cool. I've got it. But the garage…" He ran a hand over his face. "I can't remember."

"Sure you do. Fog machines coming out of abandoned cars, everything painted orange. Scarecrows crawling out of trunks and hoods. And Bella can walk with us."

He tipped his head back. "That's awesome. Thanks."

"Now you have a plan."

"Nothing I love more than a plan." Noah nodded to himself, maybe reminiscing about what used to be an Eagle's Ridge tradition. "Cool. I'll dress Bella, she'll walk with you and Will, and I can come up with a couple ideas for the garage. Perfect."

Teagan let him have a quiet moment until he looked over, more content than he had been ten minutes ago.

"I'm glad you're reopening it." She fidgeted with her purse against the arm of the love seat. "Are you going to change much?"

Noah chuckled. "You mean all the cutesy auto stuff?"

She prayed he wouldn't change the decor. "Yup, all that."

"Wouldn't dare touch a thing. My mother would never let me hear the end of it."

"Just another reason why Marlene Coleman is a good woman."

"Do you know my mom well?" he asked.

"I mostly chatted with Virginia but sometimes Marlene. They have very high opinions of the warrior in their family. Thank you for your service."

He gave a curt nod as the kids tore out the front door with Will leading the charge. "We're hungry! Can we have a snack?"

Noah hooked an arm around Bella's hip. "I'm starving!"

Knock, knock.

"Someone's at the door." Bella spun free as Will followed her to the front door.

"That'd be a delivery from my buddy's girlfriend." Noah stood up.

Teagan stood as well. "On that note, we should probably head out."

A chorus of nos came from the kids, and Teagan cut them off with a look. Bella gave Will a quick hug, then they raced out the front door.

"Hang on a second," Noah said, following them. He returned less than a minute later. "I thought Bailey was going to drop this off." He headed into the kitchen and returned. "That wasn't her. Just a delivery guy. But—" He stood next to her in the hall and shook his head. "I want to learn that trick of yours."

Teagan paused on the way to the door. "What trick?"

"The look." Noah crossed his arms and made a funny face.

She tapped his forearms. "I do not look like that."

He chuckled, uncrossing his arms and shrugging. "I don't know. I almost had it down."

"Nowhere in the neighborhood of *the look.*"

He opened the front door, and their arms brushed as he guided her out, letting his hand slide from her shoulder blade a few inches. Nothing wrong with a touch. Maybe other than the fact that it made her realize how warm his hands were— and wonder how strong they were too.

Teagan drew in a quick breath as they stood on the small front porch, watching Will and Bella spin and hop as if they might never run out of energy.

"Go hop in the car, baby," she called to Will, then she and Noah both laughed at the spectacle of them leapfrogging to her Subaru, clamoring to open the back door, and the animated discussion that ensued as Will hooked into his booster.

Noah propped an arm against a cedar pillar, leaning to her side. He wasn't in her space, but the area was small. Teagan's cheeks heated when she noticed how his muscles bunched with his arm overhead. They were close enough that his warm, woodsy cologne caught on the ever-present slight breeze, so subtle that she didn't know what made her take a quick breath until her mind registered how mouthwateringly handsome he was.

"I'll figure it out."

She snapped out of it. "What? I'm sorry…"

He deepened his smile, and sun lines at the corner of his eyes gave him a smolder. "*The look.*"

She tossed her head back. "Ha!"

"What? Too much?" Noah laughed too.

Thankful he'd turned his good looks into a smoking hot but funny moment, she had nothing but a headshake. "Bella's a doll. You'll rarely need the look."

"I still want all the weapons in my arsenal." He made grabby hands. "That's the only way this learning curve flattens."

Balling her fists loosely, she batted away his hands, like a boxer and coach practicing. "You've got this, slugger."

"Wrong sport. Rocky."

Bella trotted over and jumped up on the porch. Noah tucked her to his side. They were cute and the family resemblance strong. She rocked from heel to toe, back and forth. "Drive safely, Teagan."

"I will, Bella. Thanks for the reminder."

Noah blinked, dropping to stare at Bella.

"It's fine that she calls me Ms. Shaw at school and Teagan outside. We've known each other for too long."

"Yeah." Noah's confusion hadn't waned. "Thanks for the explanation."

"Are we leaving soon?" Will yelled from the Subaru.

"Gosh, yes." She was chatting with Noah as if they didn't

have to run to the store and knock out errands. "In a second."

"Got any other pieces of advice to share, ladybug?" Noah asked Bella.

Then it clicked. Noah hadn't seen Bella's gifted idiosyncrasies in action. It was one thing to know she was bright. It was quite another to hear her drop very adult-like statements into a conversation. Teagan winked at Noah. "I'll text you a couple tricks. Who knows if you'll ever need to throw a Hail Mary. What's your number?"

"Third sport, same conversation."

"Boxing, baseball, football." She fished it out of her purse. "I'm raising a son. I'm not clueless—though I'm positive I'd still know that if I was raising a daughter."

He rattled off his number while she had her cell in hand, then she hit Send. "Now you have me. Anything comes up, I'm always around."

Noah lifted his chin. "Appreciate that."

"And I'm off." She waved as she headed for her car.

"Now racing too?" Noah laughed.

Teagan turned but kept walking backward. "What?"

Bella giggled. "Off to the races!" Then she galloped into the front yard.

"That's a stretch." Teagan pointed at him and shook her hand, then she turned and shut Will in before opening her door to slide in the driver's seat. Teagan buckled in with a smile on her face.

"Why do you look like that?" Will asked from the backseat.

Her cheeks heated, and the grin that couldn't stop fell into hiding. "Like what? I don't look like anything." But yes she did. Had she been *flirting* with Noah Coleman? Oh, that was such a bad idea.

"Like your smile makes you smile."

Out of the mouths of babes. "Maybe it did, hon. I'm not sure."

Her text message pinged, and before she put her car into reverse, she checked it.

NOAH: *Just wondering. Did Bella say...*

NOAH: *Drive careful, Mrs. Shaw?*

NOAH: *Or*

NOAH: *Drive careful, Ms. Shaw?*

The smile that made her smile came back in full force, and Teagan glanced toward the front porch. Noah waited, watching.

Her stomach somersaulted a hundred times before she remembered to take the next breath. She tapped out "Miss."

He lifted his chin then focused on his phone, typing for a heart-stealing second before he waved good night and called Bella in. The front door shut behind them, and Teagan slipped the Subaru into reverse. Her cell phone pinged.

She drew a quick breath, daring to look.

NOAH: *Good to know. Drive safely, Miss Shaw.*

CHAPTER THREE

BAILEY'S CASSEROLE WAS in the oven, and Bella was at the table with her water bottle from school. *Smooth sailing.* Noah snapped a hand towel at her chair, and Bella laughed, trying to catch it. "All right, ladybug."

"What do we do now?"

He ran through his mental list of action items. "What do you say we clean out your backpack and pick clothes for tomorrow?"

"Now?"

When else would they do it? He had to feed her. Make sure she showered. According to every parenting blog on the internet, the key to a happy life was planning clothing the night before school. Noah had zero intention of questioning professional mothers. "That's affirmative, kid."

Bella saluted then searched over his shoulder.

"What?"

Her brown hair tipped over her face. "Is that all we're going to have for dinner?"

"Phshh. Of course not." Except, yeah. That had been his idea after the initial pizza plan got shot down. He replaced pizza with the casserole, and what else was he supposed to serve with pizza? She was short a few years for a six-pack, so this was the plan—casserole. "I was going to make…" He'd hit the grocery store but didn't have a plan. He pulled open the freezer and scowled at his options, including what his mom and aunt left. Nothing looked good as he removed the green beans to see what might be behind them. Were pizza rolls too much to ask?

"Ohh, those! Yes!" Bella bounced in her seat. "Please. With butter and salt. Please."

"The green beans?" he asked and stared at the bag in his hand like it sprouted alien arms.

"Yes!"

Okay. That was easy. Not pizza-rolls easy, but he could heat veggies. "Sure thing." He shut the freezer and twisted to the cabinet for a container. "You know, I didn't eat anything green until I was in high school. And only because coach made me."

Not finding the plasticware, he dumped the green beans into a glass bowl and perused the directions. How long was he supposed to nuke these things?

Noah pivoted and turned in the other direction, but he came up short. He put down the bag and glass bowl and double-checked the counter. What the... "Hey, ladybug?"

She tried to snap his towel, but it fell to the floor. "Yes?"

He scooped up the towel and tossed it over his shoulder. "Where's your microwave, hon?"

"We don't have one."

Noah had expected a hundred responses that revolved around her pointing out the obvious. That wasn't one of them. "Did... your grandma break it?"

"Nope. We don't have one."

"You don't have one," he repeated. "At all?"

"Never ever," Bella added. "People rush too much."

He cocked his head. "They do, huh?"

"And are they really healthy?" Bella mocked his tilted look. Noah made a mental note not to say anything he didn't want her to repeat. "Most people would say they're fine."

Bella shrugged, clearly having no idea what she was talking about.

"Okay, no microwave." He stared at the green beans, wishing like hell he could rib Lainey over her lack of a perfectly safe microwave.

Damn the irony. Cancer had taken her life before she hit her thirty-fifth birthday, and she'd done nothing but eat blueberries and avoid microwaves. Noah pinched the bridge of his nose.

"Are you feeling okay, Uncle Noah?"

His eyes sank shut. "Yeah, ladybug."

"It's healthy to be sad sometimes."

His eyes squeezed shut. "I know." Pulling in a quick breath, he turned and repeated himself, "I know."

"Teagan says so."

He ran his hand over his face. "She's right. I'm just going to…" He eyed the stove where he'd just shoved the casserole into the oven below. "Master this contraption. This is how your mom makes green beans?"

Bella giggled. "It's not a contraption. It's a stove."

"And I'm going to cook on it."

"With butter and salt."

He winked. "Got it."

After semicareful consideration, Noah dunked what looked like enough green beans, butter, and salt into a small pan. Too bad he'd torn through the stovetop directions. But how hard could it be? Heat, stir, serve.

He set the pan on the stovetop and pulled the oven open. A steamy, cheesy burst of heat rolled out. "That smells—"

"So cheesy good!"

"Agree." He flipped the hand towel over his other shoulder. "Maybe these need some water."

He threw a cup of water into the pan and snapped off the hand towel, tossing it into the drawer under the oven, then he eyed the counter. Everything seemed orderly and clean. At least his commanding officer would approve.

"Time to go do backpack and clothes."

Bella bit her lip. "Are you sure we should do that like that?"

"The clothes? Yeah."

"No, the contraption." She lowered her voice like his.

"The stove and oven will be fine."

She didn't look convinced.

"I promise."

"Oh-kay!" Then Bella skipped out of the kitchen, and Noah followed her down the hall, ready to knock more items off his to-do list like a boss.

CHAPTER FOUR

WITH EVERY EXCITED bounce from Bella down the hallway's cedar wood floors, Noah was convinced that his niece was less of a kid and more of a forty-pound lightweight. He caught up with her as she scattered the contents of her pink, green, and blue multicolored backpack on her bedroom floor and sat in the middle of an organizational nightmare.

Noah eyeballed her surroundings as if he was taking stock of a potential enemy's arsenal. Glitter hand sanitizer, a partially open lunch box, two empty snack bags, a mini hairbrush that looked as though it'd never been used. He was nearly one hundred percent certain that his mother could be blamed for the hairbrush. As if a five-year-old would be styling her hair at kindergarten—but maybe she did. He had no idea.

"Do you ever brush your hair at school?" he asked.

She glanced at the brush as though seeing it for the first time. "Nope."

"Didn't think so. Did my mom put it in there?"

"She did, but my grandma told her where my backpack was. They didn't think I could hear them."

"Thought so." He chuckled and knelt down. "Maybe next time we do this in the kitchen."

She nodded as if he'd lucked onto a fun fact, like that air was cool to breathe. "That's where we're *supposed* to do it."

"Oh." He clucked, picked up the hairbrush, and tapped it on her shoulder. "Next time, tell me."

Her eyebrows slid together as though something was on her mind, and Noah had no idea how to read that yet—or maybe he never would.

"You're not in trouble, Bella."

"I know."

"Then what's that look for?" he asked.

"Should I tell you when you aren't supposed to do things?"

Lifting a shoulder, he decided it couldn't hurt. Advice from Bella was just as valuable as advice from Teagan, given the current circumstance. He sniffed the air. Were his green beans burning? "It wouldn't hurt to share, but I might not always agree." That sounded like Teagan might approve.

He twisted toward the door, inhaling again. Something smelled burned, but he'd blackened green beans before. That wasn't the right scent. Leave it to an explosives expert to try to diagnose burned dinner by the smell.

Bella scooted closer to him. "I accept those terms."

Again with her adorable grown-up speak, and Noah set aside burned green beans and had to focus not to laugh. "Do you?"

She nodded earnestly. "I do."

He wasn't sure if half the guys on his team would say "I accept those terms." "We'll shake on it."

He held out his hand, more concerned about the acrid tinge to the air, when the smoke detector chirped. "Shoot, I'm burning the green beans!"

"I don't think you are," Bella said, following him as they hustled from her room. "You're not supposed to put anything but pans in the broiler."

Noah froze, mentally retracing his steps, then turned to

her. "What broiler?" Oh, hell. He hurried back to the kitchen and held out his hand for her to stay in the hall. "Stay put for a sec."

He reached for the hand towel on his shoulder but came up empty as he stepped to the browning green beans.

Beep.

"Freaking smoke detector," he mumbled. Where did they keep pot holders? He flicked off the top burner, scooting the crisped green beans off as they smoked. But that wasn't nearly enough to cause the haze in the kitchen.

Beep.

The casserole? How was he screwing up a simple dinner! He pulled the oven open, and black smoke billowed out. "What the—"

Then flames jumped. His dish towel! "Shoot!"

Beep.

There was a fire in the oven from the dish towel he'd tossed in below. He slammed the door shut. *Beep.* He switched the gas off and rushed to the window to throw it open and let some of the swirling air out. *Beep.* "Hey, Bella. Go open the front door."

He needed a cross draft to blow this place free of the stink. *Beep.*

"Ohhh-kay dokey."

Her giant leaps were more for fun and less for distance, and *beep,* Noah tried the oven again. The fire raged inside. He needed a fire extinguisher. *Beep.* No, he needed the fire alarm to chill. Where was that? He looked down the hall, and there was the noisemaking culprit.

He dragged the chair to the hallway, ripped the smoke detector off the ceiling, and pulled the battery out with tactical efficiency. Good to see his skills could still be put to use.

Beep.

He glared. It still had a charge even as they remained surrounded by smoke. "Go toss it in the front yard, would ya, Bug?"

She didn't miss a beat and skipped away, only to return with a report that it broke into two pieces on the sidewalk. Her lips rounded as though she were in trouble, but he couldn't have planned it better if he'd tried.

"Good work. Now to fix this—"

The distant call of fire alarm sirens brought everything to a standstill. Only in Eagle's Ridge would someone call the fire department when they heard a neighbor's fire detector and saw a little smoke out a window.

"Are they coming here?" Bella asked.

His head dropped, and slowly he nodded. "Without a doubt."

Noah turned back to the oven, and his eyes dropped to the storage cabinet underneath. But it wasn't a storage cabinet. He stomped to the sink and checked below it, where he found the obligatory fire extinguisher as the sirens blared closer.

"This wasn't on any of the mommy blogs." He pulled the broiler drawer open with his boot, and there sat the charred remains of his dish towel.

Just to be safe, he popped the pin and aimed the nozzle. There was no doubt that he'd just made the front page of the Eagle's Ridge newspaper. Then after pulling the oven open, Noah needed to douse his casserole inferno and sprayed it to a wet, white, foamy crisp.

"This is exciting!" Bella announced, perched on top of a chair.

"Riveting." The sizzling mess was completely extinguished in all of its rancid, acrid glory, and Noah turned as boots stomped into the kitchen.

Hello, Eagle's Ridge Fire Department. They entered Lainey's house—in full gear—with the man in the lead holding the broken smoke detector.

"Noah Coleman?" The man with his broken fire detector stopped in the hallway.

They even had him by name. Small town gossip at its best. "That's me. Sorry about the—"

"This is yours?" The man held up the two pieces.

"Yup." Noah crossed his arms. "I was wondering where that got to."

"I did that!" Bella piped up. "I'm sorry."

"It's fine, ladybug. Don't worry about it." Or the overreacting firemen in our house.

The word CHIEF was emblazoned on the man's jacket, and he tossed it onto the counter. "Since you're new in town—"

"Hold on a second." He *wasn't* new in town. Any embarrassment he'd had over blackening Lainey's kitchen wall and stinking the house up ceased to exist. "Let's be clear, sir. No, I'm not new in town. I was born and raised in Eagle's Ridge. My father's father was a founder, and I take great pride in that. I left for a service calling, and I'm back for a calling too. Are we clear on that?"

Their stare down was interrupted when Bella inched between them. "Am I in trouble for tampering or disabling a smoke detector device?"

"No, sweetheart."

Noah appreciated the tone the man took with Bella as she repeated the warning that she must've heard on an airplane. "I didn't catch your name."

"Fire Chief Bernie Pope."

"Good to meet you, sir. Given the circumstances." Noah

gestured. "But I think you can see everything's taken care of now."

The fire chief brushed by for his inspection as Bella chatted with a familiar face about their gear. The inspection of toasted green beans and casserole took far too long, but the man was making his point. He was in charge, and Noah had caused him to suit up and work when there was nothing to be done.

Noah softened his stance and recalibrated his approach. "Look, I'm sorry you had to come out."

The chief grunted as he took notes.

"I didn't call."

Pope shook his head. "No, your neighbor said smoke was pouring out of Lainey's house."

Wasn't that the neighbor Lainey had promised would be a helpful resource one day? "*Pouring* might've been an over-statement."

"Humph."

Noah had no idea if that was an agreement or not. "But hey, for your troubles. I just reopened Nuts and Bolts. If you or any of the guys need a tune-up, swing on by. I could use something to do, and it'll help me get the word out I'm back and opening up."

Pope chuckled. "Trust me, son. Not many don't know you're back."

What was that supposed to mean? "Then come by, any-way."

"Pretty busy." The chief took a picture with his cell phone.

Undeterred, Noah stood in his line of sight and extended his hand. "On the house."

Pope stopped, noting the intrusion in his work, and stud-ied Noah's hand. His heavy jaws worked side to side before he gave a nod. "We appreciate what you're doing for Bella." The chief met his grip, and they shook. "I'll let the guys know you're knocking twenty percent off."

"That wasn't the offer I made."

Pope pocketed his notes and phone and waved goodbye to Bella. "But it was the one that I accepted."

Noah needed the business but didn't want handouts. Then again, that was what he'd just offered. Maybe the chief felt the same way. "All right, then."

"Scrape out what you can when the oven cools. Scatter baking soda. Wet it with white vinegar and let it soak. Then attack it with elbow grease if you don't want to use chemicals, like Lainey."

"Thanks." Right now, Noah would rather rip the appliance out and start over, but he had to worry about feeding Bella. And *not* pizza because that would somehow scar her for life.

Unlike her mother, who never did anything wrong, ever—except take care of everyone and follow every rule and handle every possible concern except when it affected herself. "Don't worry. I won't douse the thing in ammonia."

Or do anything for now. Except maybe text Teagan and see how badly he'd screwed up his little ladybug.

CHAPTER FIVE

THE FIVE O'CLOCK hour at the grocery store was like social hour in Eagle's Ridge among the working moms and last-minute dinner-prepping crowd. Teagan chatted her way through produce while Will shrugged out of the polite chatter with one purpose in mind—pepperoni pizza.

Baking a frozen pizza sounded far easier than reheating last night's roast beef and potatoes. She already had salad makings at home, and the roast beef leftovers would keep for another night. Besides, somewhere at the bottom of her purse was a coupon for stuffed crust pepperoni. If that wasn't fate calling them to the frozen food aisle, Teagan didn't know what was.

A burst of colorful caftan whirled around the far end of the chilly aisle as Teagan made her way toward her son drooling over the dinner options, and she could tell by the way that Hildie Fontana gripped her colorful shawl while her mouth moved a mile a minute on a cell phone conversation, meant for all to hear, that something juicy was happening in the social boundaries of the county.

Truthfully, Teagan used Hildie as a behind-the-scenes source of useful information. She did so sparingly, but getting the dirt sometimes helped her decipher situations at school that might not be apparent.

Hildie hung up her phone, ditching it with great fanfare in her giant purse as she hooked Will for a hug before stopping in front of Teagan. "Make sure to get a chocolate chip cookie next time you're near my shop, Will. It's been a while since you've stopped by."

Teagan smiled. Hildie loved men, young and old.

The appreciation for attention went both ways. "We will!" He beamed. "Promise."

"I can't wait." Hildie was harmless, but no male in Eagle's Ridge was safe from her strings-free cookie offers. "I'll make a fresh batch if you give me a heads-up."

Will's eyes melted as wide as one of Hildie's cookies.

Even Teagan's mouth watered, and she wasn't one for sweets. "Will do."

Sufficiently appeased, Will ran back to the freezer chests and gaped at his options.

Hildie watched him press against the cold glass. "What's for dinner?"

"Pepperoni!"

"Great choice," Hildie praised. "Study all your options, because I want to chat with your mama." Her telltale eyebrows waggled.

Over the years, Teagan had decided there was a Richter scale for town gossip. The more each of Hildie's eyebrows wiggled and danced, the more newsworthy the woman found the conversation to be.

When everyone in town was curious whether Sam Tucker had noticed how Brenda Morgan had started dating again, it was the medium tempo of Hildie's eyebrows and their slight angle that clued the gossipmongers into the not-so-dramatic details of Sam falling for another girl when the money had been on Sam and Brenda to become a couple.

But Hildie's eyebrows had arched into her hairline, can-canning with every word when she recounted how Max Tucker refused to leave his house as the river flooded during Founders' Day weekend.

Right now, in the middle of the frozen food aisle, Hildie's brow action indicated that seismic activity was happening in Eagle's Ridge.

"What do we need to chat about?" At least there was no need to beat around the bush with Hildie. She wanted to share.

"Penny phoned me earlier."

Teagan shook her head. "Refresh my memory."

"Penny. She works 9-1-1 dispatch."

"Oh." Teagan wasn't sure how she felt about gossip that started with an emergency phone call. "Is everyone okay?"

Hildie swatted away her concern like a fruit fly from apples. "You are *never* going to believe what she told me."

Teagan guessed everyone was okay. If anyone had been rushed to the Coleman Center by ambulance, the conversation would have had a different tone. "What did Penny tell you?"

Hildie flapped her arms and made her multicolored caftan flair. "Well, it involves the *fire* department."

Oh, the theatrics. It was what this woman lived for, yet there were only so many things that involved a 9-1-1 call that Teagan could consider guilt-free gossip.

Teagan needed to feed Will and decided guessing might speed the conversation along. "The firehouse decided to do a calendar for charity. All proceeds go to fund your museum—"

"Oh. That would be nice." Hildie's face froze, likely lost in the innumerable poses she'd pulled in an instant. "But no."

"Do I have to guess again?" Teagan flicked a glance at her son. "Will might wither away."

Hildie snapped out of her firemen daydream and glanced at Will, pressed against the frozen food case as if he'd never seen food in his life. "No more guessing."

"Great. Give me the goods."

"The fire department is wrapping up a run to the Force house." She pitched forward. "Where Noah Coleman moved back to today!"

"What?" A little gasp caught in Teagan's throat.

"Penny said it was a double whammy while he cooked dinner."

Teagan's eyes couldn't have gotten any wider. "Are you kidding me?"

"Do I joke?" The town gossip balked then pursed her lips as though offended that Teagan had questioned the authenticity of her intel.

"I didn't mean to be rude, Hildie. It's just…" She half wanted to burst out laughing and half needed to check on Bella. "We were just there."

"Right, Will and Bella." Hildie bounced her finger, apparently remembering the friendships of kindergartners. All in the job of the town busybody. "Friends? Something more one day?"

"Never." She shook her head. "They're like siblings. But not. Would be if they could, though."

"Like the Coleman and the Stram—I mean Force—girl. I never saw Lainey as a Force. Always a Stram."

Teagan lifted her shoulder. "I didn't know Davis Force. But I do know I need to feed Will."

"You don't want to know what happened?" Hildie gaped.

Goodness, what Teagan didn't want to do was insult her again. She tried not to laugh at the thought of Noah needing the fire department while he cooked dinner. "I didn't realize you knew more details, Hildie. Sorry. What happened?"

"What happened?" Hildie repeated, flapping the shawl. "*Everything* happened!"

Hmm. Hildie was to be used only in small doses and for therapeutic purposes. A perfect student might take a nosedive before an impending divorce was announced. Hildie would know. Teagan could come up with actionable steps. But this was starting to look like chin wagging that served zero purpose. "Just the quick version. I can't forget about Will for too long."

Hildie straightened her arms in her shawl then crossed them. "*Double whammy.*"

"I got that."

"He cranked up the heat on the stovetop, but it was the oven that did him in."

Oh good gracious, would she just spit it out? Teagan glanced at Will, now opening and closing the door to the frozen pizza section. "And...?"

"He tossed a hand towel in the broiler under the oven, thinking it was a storage cabinet. *Poof.*" Hildie threw her arms in the air, and her shawl splayed brightly. "Fire."

Teagan slapped her hand over the mouth. "Oh my."

"The next-door neighbor called the fire department. Said the kitchen caught fire. Smoke was billowing out the front door and windows."

Oh God. Poor Noah. She didn't want to laugh. This wasn't funny.

"All that smoke?" Hildie shook her head. "I bet half the kitchen in that sweet cedar is gone. Just gutted. Can you imagine what it must look like? Bet the walls are black, the floors too..."

Teagan's mind wandered to Lainey's—no, Noah's— beautiful kitchen. Had he really burned it out? That would be a shame, and if so, she wouldn't laugh any more.

Hildie clucked. "Now that I think about it, maybe that was his plan."

"I'm sorry?" Teagan asked, torn from her worries.

"What better way to up his bachelor status?"

Teagan gaped. "What?"

"Very smart. Handsome man like that, one who needs help in the kitchen but who is trying? Comes from a good family with deep roots?" Hildie's voice flittered. "And have you heard his story?"

"He has a story?" Teagan's brow furrowed. This was why she didn't gossip. She didn't know if the headache pounding in her temple that very second was from irritation, aggravation, or frustration.

"He walked away from the military for Bella." Hildie tilted her head. "Bella and Will are close. Didn't you know that?"

A flash of protectiveness rushed through Teagan. Noah wasn't fresh meat for the single ladies in town to pounce on. He had much bigger things to worry about, like learning to raise a highly intelligent young girl who'd had more than her fair share of traumatic events in a short lifetime. "Yes. I'm aware he didn't re-up his contract as a Navy SEAL."

"Navy SEAL. It has a nice ring to it."

Teagan's chest pounded. "We have to go, but Hildie…"

The busybody's cell phone buzzed, and she perked up as if Prince Harry might be calling. "I have to take this."

"Sure, but hey, Hildie. Before that." Teagan stepped forward, resting her hand on the other woman's forearm. "Give him more than a day to get his bearings before you throw him to the wolves."

Hildie's smile wavered but remained strong. "You know"—she declined the call on her phone—"I forgot to pick up a new bag of chocolate chips. Can't forget that, now can I?"

Then Hildie dropped her phone into her bag, and with as much flourish as she'd arrived into the aisle, she departed.

"No problem. I have to feed Will." But Hildie was already gone, phone pressed to her ear as she hunched over, telling the latest caller of the Eagle's Ridge Fire Department run.

Teagan thought quietly about how Noah must have felt. Maybe homesick. Maybe he missed his team. The last thing he wanted was to be the center of gossip. Either way, she had come at him all wrong earlier, and he didn't need to get another round of muckraking from the rest of Eagle's Ridge.

Teagan bit her lip. Nor did she want a crew of the single and interested showing up at his door. But that wasn't why she'd said something to Hildie. Was it?

She walked over to Will as he dropped his head back and groaned. "I'm so hungry. I don't think I'm going to make it."

"Oh no. That sounds horrible." She put her pointer finger to her chin and tilted her head, humming. "Maybe we should rush home and have leftovers?"

Will snapped to like a soldier with his arms at his sides and his head facing forward. "Just kidding. I'm fine. Can we still have pizza? *Please.*"

He was such an animated kid, and he was the only guy she needed in her life. That answered her question too. Even if a smidge of interest might have been piqued—or more than a smidge—she wouldn't have kept gossipmongers from Noah just because she was interested in him.

"Which pepperoni did you decide on?"

He skipped two doors down. "I can get it! I can reach yours too!"

"Hang on." She wasn't that predictable. Sometimes she tossed it up and had thin crust or veggie.

He threw open the door and nabbed his pepperoni then correctly guessed she wanted the extra cheese–stuffed crust.

"Good choices." Her cell buzzed from the bottomless

depths of her purse. If the thing wasn't loud enough to hear, she'd forget she had it, unlike Hildie, who always had hers in her hand. Teagan silenced the notification calling for attention but spotted Noah's name.

The muscles near her collarbones tensed automatically, and Teagan flushed.

NOAH: *I'm in need of recommendations.*

"I bet." She laughed as Will tossed the pizzas into her grocery basket.

TEAGAN: *I might have some of those. What's up?*

NOAH: *Healthy. Fast. Delivery or takeout.*

TEAGAN: *For dinner?*

NOAH: *That wasn't obvious? Sorry. Yeah, for dinner.*

NOAH: *I had dinner plans. Two different plans actually. But things didn't work out the way I'd hoped.*

TEAGAN: *…I heard. ;)*

NOAH: *Really?*

TEAGAN: *Some version of what might have happened. Yeah.*

NOAH: *Man. Nothing changes in Eagle's Ridge, does it? Word still travels fast.*

"Mom? Are we leaving now?" Will bounced on his toes. Teagan pulled herself away from the cell phone.

"Why are you smiling?"

"I'm not."

"Yes, you are."

"Oh, well. I don't know, then," she stammered as heat crawled up her neck. "Let's go."

They were headed toward checkout when another text popped up.

NOAH: *Finally got everyone out of the house and about to go get takeout. Any suggestions? I'd rather sit somewhere, but I'm sure everyone at No Man's Land has heard by now.*

"Do we need anything else?" Will sidestepped across the front of the store. "Can we leave?"

"We are leaving." She quickly texted back.

TEAGAN: *So what?*

NOAH: *Hildie's coffee crew will stare and judge so they can take notes.*

Her cheeks flamed. He had no idea how dead on he was and how busted she was too. Eagle's Ridge wanted to wrap everyone in its arms but not before the town had a good gander.

"You're walking slow," Will said.

She wanted to tell him not to nag, but she was walking slowly. Texting Noah was a distraction, but every now and then, she had to use her phone. It wasn't an everyday thing.

But texting Noah wasn't work or something she *had* to do...

They moved into a short line, and she dropped the basket on the conveyor belt and her phone in her purse. "Give your mom a break every now and then, okay, big guy?"

Will leaned against her, and Teagan stroked his hair. Still, her mind wasn't one hundred percent focused. She could have invited Noah and Bella to have pizza with them tonight. Bella ate with her and Will several days a week. Maybe making that offer would be like penance for trading in gossip on what was Noah's first day on a new job. Karma was going to kick her butt if she didn't do something good—and quickly.

But her nerves jittered, and that was because she smiled at her phone when Noah's name popped up.

"Did you have library today?" she asked Will, changing the subject to one she was certain about. Kids and school.

"Yeah. We read a book where this kid was new and he sat alone at lunch and ate different foods than everyone else and no one gave him a chance and…"

Teagan's eyes shut. Was it her imagination, or did every conversation find a way to point toward Noah in some way?

"Then the other boy went over and made a friend. And they liked the food in the other lunch box. And found out new was okay and that the old kid was new to the new kid too. And…"

Teagan pulled out her cell phone, less jittery and forgetting that she thought Noah was attractive and that she'd judged him earlier.

TEAGAN: *I'm cooking pizzas if you're interested. I promise not to burn my kitchen down. You and Bella are free to come over.*

Then she held her breath. No response. The jitters resurfaced. Did she have a crush on Bella's uncle? No, that would be silly and way too quick.

"Mom?" Will inched closer to the checkout.

Why didn't Noah text back? This was ridiculous. She couldn't have a crush on someone she'd just met. But she could think he was cute. Still, Teagan gave one last hopeful stare at her phone and willed a yes reply to appear.

Nothing.

A hollow knot of disappointment burrowed itself into her stomach. That hadn't been there in a long time. She placed the two pizzas on a conveyor belt and tucked the basket underneath as they waited on the woman in front of them.

There could be many reasons he didn't write back. Maybe

he was driving to eat already. Or perhaps she'd been too judgmental when they first met, and he didn't want to have dinner with her and Will.

Ping.

The text message notification brought a barrel of anticipation that Teagan wanted to ignore. There were too many parents and friends who might send a text, but there was no reasoning with the swarm of fluttering butterflies racing through her veins.

Teagan swiped her phone's screen and saw his name then two words.

NOAH: *Sounds good.*

She rocked back on her heels, biting down a smile. "Hey, Will? Run and get two more pizzas."

He didn't have to be told twice to run free in the grocery store. The kid blasted to the frozen food aisle almost as quickly as her heart raced now that Noah and Bella were joining them for dinner.

Another text popped up.

NOAH: *If it's not a problem. No pity meals for us.*

A pity meal? Who was he kidding? Of all the reactions she might have had since Hildie had dropped the kitchen firebomb, pity wasn't on the list.

TEAGAN: *We'll be home in 20. Pizza will be on the table in 45 minutes.*

She pinged her home address to him as Will came back with two more pizzas and tossed them onto the conveyor belt. Teagan pulled out her store coupon for frozen pizza and chewed on the inside of her cheek as they were rung up and she paid.

NOAH: *Pizza, huh? I have a funny story to tell you.*

Since they hadn't walked the short distance from their home to the grocery store, they didn't need a bag for their pizzas. She and Will carried two boxes each to her Subaru as he hopped along the edge of the sidewalk and she wondered how pizza might be funny.

CHAPTER SIX

"DO YOU EVER stop bouncing?" Noah made overexaggerated head motions that followed Bella's jumps as he held her hand.

"Not really." It was as though she had springs on the bottom of her shoes, bounding with every step. "Mommy wanted to bottle me up."

He squeezed Bella's hand as she hopped toward Teagan's front door. "She'd have made a killing."

Bella stopped abruptly. "Mom didn't kill anyone. She said you did sometimes. But they were bad guys. But she died and wasn't killed. That's different than a homicide, did you know that?"

Noah's lips parted, and he was unsure where to start. Suddenly he felt more out of place than he had thirty seconds ago, and he hadn't known that was possible. He didn't have a clue how to talk to Bella, much less raise her. If this was the kind of situation they'd find themselves in on her best friend's front sidewalk, what would happen when life really got tough?

Noah cleared his throat. "Make a killing, er. It's like an expression. It means to do well."

"Oh," Bella perked up. "Like an idiom."

"Uh, yeah. Sure." More like he was an idiot. Idiom? Was there a Google Translate option for "smart kid"?

"Like a penny for your thoughts?"

"I think so." He didn't know what constituted an idiom.

"People I don't know say that to me when I don't want to talk to them."

Noah crouched down. "I get that. A lot. It comes with being in the military. Sometimes there are things that I saw or thought that I had to process on my own or with someone who saw the same things as me, and when others ask me to talk about it? They'd never be able to relate." He shrugged. "I never knew what to say."

"Are you sad my mom is gone?" she asked quietly.

He nodded then scooped her into his arms before walking on his knees to the first step on Teagan's porch. "Yup, ladybug."

"Does it hurt your insides?"

He kept nodding but this time made the motion bigger. "Sure does." Then he kissed the top of her head. "What about you?"

"People I don't know cry in front of me, and it makes me feel uncomfortable."

Hmm. "Why?"

"They act like they want to make me feel better. But they want the consolation."

"Consolation, huh?" he asked quietly. "Big word with big meaning."

She leaned against him. "But it's true." Bella perked up, excited. "It adds insult to injury."

He had to laugh, despite the topic. "Worked in an idiom there, huh?"

"Yeah." She nodded quickly. "That was one, right?"

"I think so. But we'd probably have to ask your English teacher if it's an idiom or a, I don't know, cliché, or a phrase—"

"I don't have an English teacher," she said.

"You don't?" His forehead bunched. "*Right*. Because you're in *kindergarten*."

"I have reading workshop," Bella added.

As if they were discussing semantics in kindergarten. Or maybe they were. He had no clue. "Look, back to your mom. I'm always here, and I'm always going to get you."

"Because you love her."

"Yup."

"She was like my twin, like your grandma and my dad. Lainey and I did everything together."

"Like me and Will."

"Maybe so." He gave her a squeeze. "Anything else we should touch on before we go inside?"

Bella leaned back, deep in thought. "Yes."

"What's that?"

"You should know that there's a spot under the staircase. That's the best hiding place. And Will's room is cooler than mine. His pillows have arms that sit up by themselves. He can beat me eating more peanut butter crackers. *But* I can outdrink him in a water contest."

For all the words and *idioms*, she was just a little kid. "I'll teach you a couple tricks. You can take him in peanut butter crackers in a month. Easy."

"You sound like my mom." She wrapped her tiny arms around him. "Love you."

Then Bella popped up and rushed through the front door as he pushed off the stairs.

He rubbed his sternum, his mind heavy with the past as much as the present, as he followed Bella's path up the front porch stairs.

But it wasn't just discussing Lainey that had his chest knotted. Anxiety had unfurled the moment he turned his dually over and backed the truck out of the garage. About what, though? Teagan?

"We're—" He stepped into the warm hallway as Will whooshed past Noah, grabbing Bella in his wake. "Here."

When Noah looked over from the tailspin that was two quick kids, he was face-to-face with one beautiful and very in-the-know Teagan. And if her face wasn't trying to hide that she'd heard the gossipy details of a fire that had to have been blown out of proportion, Noah might've gaped a little longer at the sexy slide of her oversize sweater, draping off one shoulder. Hell, his mind would've wandered more than it was. For as modestly as she was dressed, her curves weren't well hidden, and his palms itched to learn how soft her sweater was. How quickly it would slide up off her torso and over her head.

Standing alone in the hall with a single mother who'd just saved his butt, he took a deep breath. He only half admitted to himself that she looked hotter in fuzzy socks and skinny jeans than the women he saw the last time he went on leave, chasing high heels and a short skirt.

Teagan had both hands wrapped around a mug, and she took a sip from it before she nodded him inside. "Careful, or they might plow you over."

"I can take it."

She led the way toward the kitchen, past a staircase where he eyed the *best hiding spot ever* and heard her laugh. "No comment."

He chuckled as well, breathing in the mouthwatering smell of melting cheese and baking dough. "I can only imagine what you heard."

She put the mug on the counter. "I can only imagine the entire back side of the house is gone."

He coughed out a laugh. Even that was a bit much for

town gossip. "Man, that story grew legs. The town chatterbox-es don't play around."

"Hildie at her best."

He snorted softly. "I know Hildie."

Teagan stepped to the side, waving him in. "A handsome guy like you? Of course you know who she is, because she knows who you are."

Handsome. He smiled. *Again*. As though he was the kid who left Eagle's Ridge fresh out of high school and hadn't had years of seasoning to cool his reaction to the pretty girl smiling at him.

Teagan's house was almost as Bella had described it. Based on how much fun she'd said she had there, Noah half expected to see slides coming through the walls and tic-tac-toe boards painted on the floors. It was decidedly Northwest and fresh. Natural wood and windows and the green from the outdoors met his gaze in every direction. "Nice place. I had visions of a carousel."

She checked the oven's timer. "Why's that?"

"This is her favorite place *ever*."

Teagan grinned. "Will would say the same about your place. Please don't burn the rest down."

"You've got jokes." He took a seat on a barstool at the counter that divided the kitchen and dining area. "It feels off to call Lainey's place mine."

She picked up her mug, but instead of sipping from it, Teagan held it toward him.

"Are you offering me your drink?"

"Nope." She laughed.

His eyes dropped to the mug. Giant tacos with a range of emotional faces decorated the face of it, and in the middle was scrawled WANNA TACO BOUT IT? He raised his chin.

"Really?"

"If this mug doesn't get you talking, I can find a new one." She cocked an eyebrow and turned to a cupboard. "Speaking of which, do you want tea? It's decaf."

"I'm good, thanks."

Teagan placed an empty mug in front of him. "Then you can just keep it by you for now."

He picked up a mug showing a Lego man lying on a Lego bed, talking to a Lego shrink with a thought bubble. *I keep having this dream that my feet are stuck. I can't move. Nothing around me changes.* "If this is a psychological test or trick to get me to open up about my feelings, I rebuke you."

She laughed. "Just calling it like I see it. *Stubborn.*"

"I just had an intense moment on your front porch. I'm emo'ed out for the moment."

Teagan paused. "Bella's okay?"

"I remind her of Lainey, apparently." Noah cracked a smile. "That and she schooled me in grammar, SAT words, and *idioms* between the time we left my front door and walked through yours. I had to do something to assert my... relevance?" He winked.

"If she's talking to you, you're relevant."

Maybe that was what he should have gathered from their heart-to-heart about people she didn't know and their consolations.

The timer buzzed, and Teagan grabbed mitts and opened the oven. A burst of heat and savory-scented goodness rolled through the kitchen.

"That smells great."

She slid the bottom rack out and removed two small pizzas.

"Can I help?"

She gave him a funny look then turned back to the top rack. "I've got it."

"What?"

"I've got it." Teagan slid the pizzas onto the counter, and ding, ding, he remembered that Eagle's Ridge gossip said he might never live down his kitchen incident.

"I didn't burn down that house." He scoffed. "Not a single wall is singed. Maybe let Hildie know."

Teagan tossed her oven mitts on the counter. "It's your house now."

"What'd I say?"

"That house."

Noah shrugged. It was Lainey's house.

Teagan walked to the counter bar and leaned on the end. "You'll find a way to change it from that house to *your home*."

Would he?

"If you don't believe me..." She mimicked his shrug in a playful manner that made her bare shoulder dip out of the oversized knit sweater. "Get through today and then talk to me again."

Teagan turned back to the pizza and pulled out a slicer from a drawer, leaving him to his thoughts. His aunt and mom had decided along with Lainey that it would be best for Bella to stay in the house she grew up in, and he wholeheartedly agreed with their decision. But now it felt funny to live there.

"House, home." He pushed off the barstool and went over to help. "I see what you did there."

"I figured out you weren't a fool." Teagan pointed at a cabinet. "Plates are in there."

"On some things." Noah grabbed four and followed her gaze to another cabinet and found glasses. "Roger that."

A minute later with his hands full, he found peace in setting the table. Some things never changed, whether he laid out forks and knives at home in Eagle's Ridge or doled out plates and glasses with teammates in a foreign land during downtime on a classified mission.

When he was finished, Teagan had a salad in a bowl on the table and pizzas as the centerpiece, ready to serve.

"Not bad, partner." She lifted her hand to give him a high five.

"It's been a rough afternoon, but I'm not fragile," he cracked. "No coddling needed."

She raised an eyebrow. "You don't have to assume I'm coddling." She didn't drop her raised hand, instead wiggling it for attention. "But if you protest too much, I'll assume you're in desperate need of pampering."

He chuckled. "Point made." He slapped her much smaller hand, and as their fingers brushed, his palm tickled with an urge to clasp her hand.

"Hungry?" She pulled her hand away quickly and shoved both fists into her jeans pockets, pivoting toward the steaming pizza.

He didn't like how quickly she split. "Hey."

"Hmm?" Teagan rocked on her heels, barely glancing his way.

"Thanks. You could give me so much hell right now, and it's cool you're not."

Slowly, she stopped the heel rock. "I—"

A thunder of footsteps blew into the room, followed by a chorus of "We're hungry!"

Teagan ushered them toward the sink. "Hands! Wash those hands."

Whatever she had been about to say was gone.

Will and Bella shared a stool in front of the water faucet,

making a mess more than killing germs, while Teagan filled glasses with milk—including some for him, which he got a kick out of—then they sat around the table as though they each had assigned seats.

The kids took the middle of the rectangular dining table, and Teagan headed toward the far end, leaving a vacant end chair for him.

At that moment, he realized he was the stranger in the room. He didn't know *his* seat, and he was aware both kids had better table manners than half the men he knew.

Guilt needled him in the ribs. Noah barely knew Bella beyond FaceTime, mailed cards, and the rare holiday visit. He loved her with every beat of his heart, but knowing who the kid was, that was different, and sitting at this table... No, they didn't make him feel like a stranger. More like a friend. Both old and new.

They waited for him to sit. Noah rubbed his chest, rolled his shoulders back, and pulled out the chair at the head of table. The second his butt touched down, Bella and Will chattered with food requests, their unsteady hands reaching for pizza.

He smiled, not expecting this, though he had zero expectations. Literally, none.

He hadn't put one iota of thought into whether Bella might have table manners or whether Lainey had served meals with... What was a good word? *Purpose.*

"Salad?" Teagan asked.

"Thanks." Noah took the large bowl Will shoved his way, passing it toward his niece.

Both kids acted as if they were famished, but they didn't shovel the dinner down their throats. Again, Noah knew adults who made more of a mess, and it reminded him of something he had learned on surviving hell week, that meals were solely for consuming calories. Protein and nutrition were secondary while on the job.

He ate his salad in quiet, listening to Bella and Will recount the harrowing drama of the fire drill, and when he had a break, he motioned to the table. "This is really nice, Teagan."

"Nothing, really. We're glad you're both here."

"I'm always here," Bella added.

"Doesn't change that I like having you at my table, sweet pea."

Noah swallowed another mouthful of lettuce and tomato and suddenly missed Lainey. This was her chair, her daughter, the conversation she was supposed to hear. She was his confidant, and he was her hero. Wasn't that how they'd always been? Not twins but always wanting to be. Closer than just the sister that she wasn't, even. Cousins could be that close, and that stabbing in his chest wouldn't go away.

"What'd you do today?" Bella asked him.

He took a quick breath. "Stopped by Nuts and Bolts."

"Is it open yet?" Teagan asked.

"Soon."

"I want to drive a tractor." Will dropped his fork. "Can you show me?"

Noah lifted a shoulder. "I don't have a tractor. But if I did, I could show you."

"Told ya," Bella said.

"It's an automotive shop," Teagan explained to Will. "The one you liked to visit."

Will perked up. "With all the cool stuff?"

Noah smiled. "You got it. I've kept all that too."

"Awesome."

Bella and Will kicked their legs under the table, giggling,

and stopped upon one swift look from Teagan. Noah really needed to master that drop-chin-and-pinch-eye thing she did. He was ninety-nine percent sure that if he tried it, a kid would cry.

"Which type of pizza looks good?" Teagan asked, this time in a normal volume.

Noah eyed the choices and realized eating with kids was a lot like eating with the guys. If he didn't hop to, he'd go hungry. "That one."

"Good choice."

As Teagan moved to dole the slice, Will's hand shot forward. "I want to help."

"Sure thing, buddy." Noah lifted his plate and caught the flying slice of pizza at the last second.

Bella ate her pizza backward, and Will ate his topping-side down. They both had pizza sauce on their faces and ranch dressing on their chins. Noah laughed, settling back in his chair and taking a sip of milk.

"What's funny?" Bella asked.

"Just taking it all in, ladybug."

Bella and Will were having a heated debate on whether honeysuckles had honey in them, and Noah caught Teagan studying him.

"Are you okay?" she mouthed.

Good question. He ran a quick hand into his growing hair and nodded. But the truth was that this dinner table was nothing that any parenting blog or new-to-guardianship checklist had prepared him for. He was content to see and hear the clatter and chatter as napkins dropped and milk sloshed.

Noah was a planner. He understood the planks of success and why he was driven to always triumph. He liked to win. It took resources. Prep. Training.

That was how he approached moving back to Eagle's Ridge and taking over Bella's care. Every resource he'd consulted had mentioned the immense risks that he'd come across, but none explained the reward other than the joys of parenting. What the hell was that?

This was *that*. His chest tightened. Was he okay? "I'm doing all right."

"Good. Bella, seconds?" Teagan offered Bella more salad, only to receive a polite ranch-dressing-covered headshake, then she caught his eye again. "Don't forget to eat. You're just starting this marathon."

He appreciated the good-natured mothering as he promised to do as told. This was the life. Good food. Great company. Maybe he was doing better than all right tonight.

CHAPTER SEVEN

T HE PIZZAS HAD been demolished. Even the salad had been eaten to the bottom of the bowl, and since both of Teagan's helper bees were on cleanup duty, the kids had piled utensils and cleaned off the table as best they could. Warm water ran over Teagan's hands as she washed off the dishes that Noah had scraped, and the two adults worked side by side in silence and listened to Will and Bella question each other over who had counted closer to infinity.

Will stopped volleying incoherent numbers and, at the foot of the table, called, "Can we go watch a movie?"

The table was cleared, and Bella waited patiently next to Will. Teagan was fine with it, but she decided to ask Noah too and lifted her eyebrows his way. He snickered as though he thought she was nuts for asking, then Teagan gave the kids a thumbs-up. "Finish what you were watching the other day."

As soon as they were out of the room, she wondered if he needed a reminder that he was in charge. Will led the way to the living room—and stopped, turning back. "Noah? Where are your kids?"

"Me?" Noah wiped his hands on a kitchen towel.

"He has me now," Bella added.

"Good point, ladybug."

Ladybug. Cute. "Will, leave Mr. Coleman alone."

"Ya know." He turned to her, pressing his lips together.

"The mister part is weird for me. Maybe it's an adjustment thing..."

She shrugged. "Your call."

"Just Noah."

"*Noah*," Will tried out. "Why don't you have kids?"

Teagan tittered. "And that part doesn't make you uncomfortable?"

He cracked a grin. "Nope." Then he walked back to the dining table and spun a chair around to straddle it. "Because my old job kept me away from home a lot, and then I never found anyone I wanted to have kids with."

"How do you have your kids?" Will followed up.

Noah's mouth opened and closed, and he sent a silent SOS to Teagan.

As much as she'd enjoy seeing Noah struggle with that one, she wanted to handle the birds and the bees on her own. Preferably with the right info, and who knew what he'd have to offer to the kindergarten crowd. "Time for the movie. Now or never, please."

Neither Will nor Bella seemed to notice Noah squirming as they left for the living room.

Noah clucked his tongue. "I may never be able to thank you enough for saving me from myself at that moment."

She shooed that away. "Like I'd let you get within ten miles of that conversation."

"Hey." He stood up from the chair, spinning it back to the table. "If I had to, I'd nail it."

His footsteps were slow. Mesmerizing. They seemed far louder than they actually were in the quiet kitchen, where there was no sound to compete other than the thump of her heartbeat. Noah had a way about him when he walked. It wasn't a swagger. More of a stroll that oozed confidence and breathed dominance. Her gaze flitted away instead of focusing on his broad chest and thick arms. It wouldn't be right to stare at the hardened edge of his jawline, not when his full lips made her wonder what his kiss might feel like. Teagan needlessly rearranged the salt and pepper shakers on her counter. Fidgeting was far better than imagining his take on the birds and bees.

"Teagan?"

The pepper clinked into the salt. Her cheeks pinked when she gripped their tops to steady her hands. She coolly lifted her gaze as though he wasn't working through her mind in ways that caused a hot flash. "Hmm?"

He stopped on the other side of the breakfast bar. Three feet of polished wood countertop, her favorite part of the kitchen, separated them.

"Nothing to say?" He smoothed his large hands across the well-cared-for wood, following the grain. "Haven't known you that long, but you always have something on the tip of that tongue."

A shiver slid down her spine, and he held her eyes. Teagan swallowed, unsure why she was unnerved. "Nailing things. That's my concern."

Amused, he crossed his arms, doing nothing to bat away the images in her head of how this man could nail any woman he wanted. His long-sleeve Henley molded to the curves of his biceps, and the partially open buttons at the top of his collar stretched, taunting her with what lay beneath. "Why do you think I'm going to screw up?"

"I didn't say that."

He squinted, unbelieving. "Yeah, you did. Almost word for word."

She couldn't exactly tell him that she assumed bachelor

Navy SEALs who looked like him didn't have a good handle on the correct words and the point of sex, at least from the perspective of a five-year-old.

He laughed. "I mean, I know why I think I screw up, but what about you?"

Well, ugh... "I'm not sure."

He stepped around the breakfast bar, and her pulse quickened. It wasn't as if they hadn't been alone, and of course, she'd had any number of sex-related conversations with parents. Even attractive dads, but at the time it never occurred to her that they were good-looking. Sometimes it was just a fact. A person was attractive, and she went about her business.

This was... chemistry. They had it. Noah walked closer, and his skin prickled with nerves and excitement. Their tension stacked, compounding with the hours they had known each other and with every inch they drew closer.

Teagan's insides fluttered. The dizzy race of blood at the base of her neck made her breath stutter, then he stopped. Too close to be near her and too damn far away.

Noah leaned his elbow on the counter. "I don't buy that for a second, Ms. Shaw."

Okay. Okay. That was flirting. Noah was flirting with her? But nothing about the gravity of the situation drawing them together seemed strained by her ridiculous bachelor-SEAL-on-the prowl assumptions.

Heat curled up her neck, and she didn't know what to say or think anymore.

"You don't trust me." He angled closer, but it was the devastating smile that closed the distance, almost curling around her.

Teagan licked her lips, concentrating on the even keel of her tone. "I didn't say that."

"You didn't have to."

She snorted at the smug confidence. That much she could do without worry. Teasing him was easy. "Did the SEALs give you the power to read minds?"

He inched back, and their moment broke. Teagan could almost picture a heavy bubble bursting, the soap splashing and flying every which way in the sun, and she was the one to pop it. He'd flirted. She'd assessed. Rebuked. Thrown a bit of sarcasm on top of the wariness she'd burdened him with earlier. After school, that had been about Bella. Now?

Teagan turned toward the wood counter, smoothing her hands as he had done from the other side.

"I'm sorry someone gave you a reason to be this defensive," Noah said quietly.

Her splayed hands froze, and the "I'm not" didn't make it past her lips because he was correct. Noah had been flirting with her, and she'd slammed him away. What started as a parenting discussion had turned into a far more intimate conversation, and without crossing any lines, but it was now... nothing.

Teagan turned back to the empty sink rather than talk about her ex-husband, and Noah quietly drummed his fingers on the counter. "I wasn't trying to pry."

She turned on the water for no good reason. The dishes were mostly done. Just a few left to load, and they could be finished tomorrow or after company left.

"I know." She stared out the window into her dark back-yard, past the insulated shed and a fence line break to the pine trees that backed her neighborhood.

The finger drumming stopped, and Noah moved to her side, arm to arm. Silently, he grabbed a dish that she'd scraped and sprayed earlier and loaded it into the dishwasher. Teagan glanced over at him, and he dropped a quiet smile to her. They went to work without a word. She scraped off the crumbs and sprayed away the cheese stuck to the plates before handing them to him. He stacked them, grabbing the glasses and lining them on the top row while she scratched baked-on cheese off a pizza stone.

When the dishwasher was full, she filled the soap cup and put the detergent back under the cabinet as Noah shut the door.

Teagan pressed the button for normal wash then dried her hands on the towel Noah passed to her before she tossed it to the side. "My ex-husband was a treasure-hunting con artist."

"Interesting profession."

She smiled. Not the normal response. "He was always busy, always promising riches even as he bolted at a moment's notice."

She lifted a shoulder to indicate that she didn't know what her ex had done. Didn't care, either, but maybe that was too callous to share. "The only trip I ever joined him on was to Alaska, and we didn't do much treasure hunting."

Noah made a face.

Teagan blushed deeply. "No! I mean, he ran into friends he knew, and they left me to enjoy the wilderness for a few days by myself. Just as well."

"Weird to run into friends in Alaska."

"His friends were probably weird to begin with. They were the type to spend months scouring the Bay of Bengal or the South China Sea for riches."

"Is that even legal?" He scoffed.

"No idea. Didn't matter because there were never riches found."

His brown eyes softened. "You don't seem like someone to

fall for the wanderlust type."

"I thought he was eccentric, and"—she rolled her eyes—"I'm sure half this town still does. He blew in like a storm with tales of adventure, but I think he used me to have a home base."

Noah's lips flattened. "Hate you were used for anything."

"I don't hate it. Or anything. Realizations like Spence—Spencer, that's his name—when you figure out that someone doesn't love you and married you for a mailing address… It's one of those things you go through, so you can grow through it. Something better is waiting for me on the other side one day."

"I like that." Noah leaned back as though he were turning that over, then he nodded. "That's a good one."

"Helps when it's your job to figure out how to handle road bumps."

"An ex-husband is a road bump?"

"Maybe roadkill." She made a face. "Well, he's still alive, but at that same level, dirtbag. Pardon my language."

His mouth twitched. "I've heard worse."

"Spence wasn't into the idea of marriage. I'm not sure why I thought things would be different with a baby."

The gleam in Noah's eyes vanished. "Wasn't a good dad?"

"Was never a dad. One look at a pregnancy test, and he split." Teagan sighed. "Will wasn't an accident, and I don't know what I expected. But…"

Noah came closer, comforting her with a hand on her shoulder and a light squeeze. "Seems like you're being hard on yourself."

Her eyes slipped shut. In one simple moment, his palm copped her shoulder and the weight of her body wanted to lean into him. Her family wasn't close, and Teagan had moved to

Eagle's Ridge for the great job opportunity in the school system. She stayed for the tight-knit community. But she didn't have the closeness of a casual hug whenever she wanted, not that she had thought much about that need.

Sighing, she nodded, agreeing with him somewhat. "Maybe just annoyed. Everyone who knows Spence still thinks back to our marriage as though I married a fun guy who wasn't meant to be tied down. It's annoying, and it's an excuse."

Noah's hand dropped, taking away its protective warmth. "It says something about society, honestly."

Caught off guard, she hesitated. "What do you mean?"

"If a mother ran off to go hunt for treasure?" He shook his head. "She'd be roasted. I'm not sure how treasure pays in child support—"

"It doesn't. He has no legal or financial responsibility."

He leaned against the counter. "I can see why you're careful."

Careful... Very. Except with Noah. She'd told him more about herself than she'd told anyone. Teagan bit her lip. "About earlier, and every time today that I've stuck my foot in my mouth. I didn't know you, but I know Lainey wouldn't have put Bella in a bad situation."

"You can stop explaining any time, Teagan."

She dropped her head then looked back at him. "Okay, it was all for Bella's best interest. More than mine, whatever defensive walls I may have."

The corner of his soft brown eyes tightened. "You wouldn't be half the woman you are if you didn't protect those kids."

It wasn't just his compliment but how he said it. Earnest and soft. Thoughtful, as if each word cast a net around her, pulling her closer to hear more. "Thanks."

"And, I can scale any *wall*." There wasn't a hint of innocence behind that SEAL's smile. "Now that I know the history behind it? Doesn't worry me at all."

The air in the kitchen thinned. He stood, rugged and charming, laying on the line far more than she understood, and he was forward. Aggressive and charming, unlike Spence, who was just a charmer. But forward how? Noah hadn't said a thing. Hadn't made a move. She couldn't breathe as fireworks threatened to ignite the air around them, and Noah hadn't even hugged her. Not so much as a kiss, and nowhere near an inappropriate suggestion.

"You know the right things to say." A fever smoldered under her skin.

His face searched hers. "How so?"

"I'm not sure. But..." They were two grown adults in the midst of a full-fledged moment where her breaths didn't feel deep enough and her mind swam in warm circles. "I really like talking to you."

"I..."

Did his skin feel hot like hers? Would his fingers grip her as tightly as his eyes promised he might hold her? She stepped closer, her hair falling across her face, and he didn't move. His jaw tensed. His shoulders shifted back as his nostrils flared with a deep inhale.

What was she doing? She was too close! Her words were too intimate! Teagan's cheeks blazed almost as hot as the sea of embarrassed tears that taunted her eyelids.

She was a helper. He needed help. Simple!

They had a friendly connection, and now she'd taken advantage of that.

"I am so sorry." Teagan turned to the sink, hating the realization that she'd disclosed too much and the cold sweep rushing through her chest with the new space between them. "That was inappropriate."

In all her years as a counselor, she had never taken advantage of a situation, and that was what she had just done. Humiliated, Teagan didn't know what was worse. Rejection tonight, having to face Noah time and time again in the future, or knowing that she'd poured her heart out about the kids as her priority then almost made a move on Noah on his first day as Bella's primary caretaker.

The dishwasher chugged. Teagan counted its rotations instead of focusing on the man who didn't move from beside her. They both waited until the dishwater changed to a different cycle, and he gripped her bicep, gently swinging her in front of him. "Stop apologizing to me. We haven't done anything wrong."

We haven't.

Not her or him but *we*, and that was because of him.

"Fine." She forced a half smile onto her face, though her embarrassment was no less. Her gratitude, however, soared. She should have known the moment he walked up and shook her hand. Noah Coleman was a gentleman.

CHAPTER EIGHT

I F NOAH COULD survive BUD/S when he was naïve and too young to know how hard life could be, then he could survive an innocent evening with Teagan Shaw while she was wearing what had to be the cutest, comfiest, most form-fitting outfit known to man. He didn't even have a foot fetish, but he'd already spent too much time focusing on how he'd pull those damn fuzzy socks off her feet.

Every part of him ached, and not in a way that he might've thought when it came to a woman he wanted and didn't know if he should touch.

Scratch that. He'd never met a woman he didn't know if he should touch. Noah had high standards. He wasn't anywhere close to sainthood, but he made picky guys look as if they'd dive into an all-you-can-handle buffet of debauchery. So he knew quickly who might interest him. Looks played a role, but the number one quality for someone driving him wild was heart. Passion. A dedication to whatever made their world rock.

Teagan had that in droves, and she had that about something he cared about too. Bella. Will. The children she worked with.

There was no question that they had a mutual attraction, but she'd easily set that aside to make sure Bella was taken care of. He'd never met a woman like her before, and Noah didn't know what he should do.

Now he questioned everything, and that was an unfamiliar situation. Uncertainty wasn't acceptable. A measure of risk was allowed, but not unexpected uncertainty, and he'd pulled back hard and fast, needing to reassess his motives.

But with that half-appeased grin and ambiguous eyes on a woman he needed to kiss, Noah could've kicked his own butt from here back to Washington, DC.

Kissing Teagan in the middle of her kitchen… He inhaled again, wanting to calm the need racing through him. But breathing wouldn't do anything when he wanted the taste of her tongue on his. He couldn't help grinding his molars now that he'd blown his chance to slide his hands along her back.

"The kids are quiet," she said, punting the subject far away from his sexy thoughts of her in that sweater and those jeans.

He shifted his weight. "Must be a good movie."

"They've only seen it a hundred times."

Noah would have moved a mountain to take away her awkward blush and replace the color with cheeks aflush from kissing.

Maybe she needed a minute. "I'll go check on the kids."

Then Teagan could do whatever women did when they wanted to ignore a man and recalibrate. His fingers were crossed that she couldn't see he needed a five-minute reprieve as well. His arousal might be poisoning his objectivity when it came to her.

"Sounds good." She didn't glance his way, reaching for Will's lunch box.

Hell, who could blame her? He'd just spent the night hitting on her. There was crossing the line, then there was how he did life—big and bold. Not smart when there were two uncommonly quiet kids to take into account.

He left Teagan and her lunch making then headed toward the sound of the movie. He rounded the corner of the living room and stopped short, cracking a smile. Will and Bella were conked out and propped against each other in front of the television.

He crept a few inches into the living room, taking advantage of their stillness, and stood to study the kids. Amazing how both looked so much younger. How could these two tiny people produce so much noise and energy? He focused on Bella and her soft brown hair and angel's skin.

If he screwed this up, the consequences would be epic—and tragic. The calamity of screwing up was much bigger than any parenting blogger could articulate in the crash-course of blog posts he read on flights overseas and links that his family had sent him.

Little strands of Bella's brown hair lifted when she sneezed, and she scrubbed them off her face, not waking up or falling from the precarious position where she and Will balanced.

"Hey." Teagan brushed his forearm. "Oh," she whispered then nodded back to the hall after an exchange of silent looks.

He leaned against a bar area on the cedar wall across from the living room's entryway, and she remained straight as an arrow. Noah sighed. "I'll scoop her up and be out—"

"Sure." Teagan gave a smile that must have made a thousand PTA meeting appearances. It was welcoming, safe, and surface level. He hated it. "Unless you have questions on school or kid stuff. Then let the kids sleep, and I can answer your questions."

Her voice was firm and even. Helpful. He wished that he could feel the texture and pause that she put into every heartfelt thought. Noah licked his lips, looking away, understanding why she'd gone formal and wanted to reestablish their boundaries. That didn't mean he liked it.

"Mm-hmm," he grunted and ground his back into the cedar planks.

Teagan watched him for a second longer than he guessed she might've. Then, posture perfect—even in her casual clothes—she pivoted to face the kids, a picture of unmoved beauty. He held in a laugh. Here he was grunting and moping, and she could pull off being a smarmy teacher in fuzzy socks.

Fuzzy socks and an oversized sweater that taunted him with a bare shoulder. Add thick brown hair that could've passed for red in the right light, and he could've grumbled too.

Teagan turned, casting her amber eyes on him—him, but not his eyes. Barely his face, and he was tired of this already. Not fifteen minutes had passed.

"Teagan?"

Her eyes lifted to his. Finally.

"Back in the kitchen—" He lost her eyes, and no, that wasn't how this was going to happen. Noah pushed off the wall, and her gaze jumped back to his as he stepped close. "I made you feel uncomfortable, and I'm kicking my ass for that."

Those beautiful golden eyes widened. "What? No."

"I did. You don't have to be polite." He gave his most earnest smile. "I said too much, and you've gone above and beyond. Not just Bella. But me." He let the fake smile melt away and leaned close. "I'd really like to not screw that up on my first day."

Her pink lips parted, holding back for a curious moment. "What are you talking about?"

He laughed, looking away then back. "I hit on you."

"No, you didn't. Not really."

"*You wouldn't be half the woman.* It wasn't meant to be a line, I swear, and I get how it might've come off like that.

Sorry."

She balked. "I didn't think it was a line, and Noah?"

"What?"

"I hit on you."

There it was. The texture. That sound. The breathy anticipation of what might be. Her confession. Again, Teagan's cheeks pinked, but this time, Noah cared a lot less, because she had that thing between them back in her voice. It was decipherable only by him, and he liked the way it tightened his lungs and made the muscles in his back strain.

Noah drew in a slow breath, searching for the right words. But they didn't come. Who knew what those were supposed to be when they'd gone through the heartache that had pitched them together.

"Teagan." He pressed them forward until her back met the cedar wood wall. "I have no idea what I'm doing."

Her chin tilted up, her lips parting with tiny breaths he wanted to capture with a kiss.

"And that's foreign to me." He towered over her, but he gave her enough space that she could roll away, plenty of room so he could take in more than just her face. But she smelled like flowers. Not sweet but strong and wild. Noah ducked his cheek to hers, brushing his lips close to her ear.

Her palms smoothed the front of his Henley. Not pushing away, not grabbing for more.

Together they were back at the same line as in the kitchen earlier. The one they'd both eased away from. But this time they toed the line, savoring and wondering, testing whether the Do Not Cross was a figment of their imagination, a simple cautionary tale that they'd concocted for no good reason, or if hormones and arousal were calling the shots.

Teagan slid her cheek against his mouth, and he stifled a

groan.

"Neither do I," she whispered. "No clue."

He chuckled quietly, leaning his weight against her. "It'd be easier if one of us knew."

Pressed between them, her fingernails scratched down his stomach, and he nuzzled his nose against her neck, breathing against her skin and memorizing how she smelled. Teagan's soft murmurs made the hairs on the back of his neck stand, and he let his lips drift to her cheek.

"I'm going to kiss you on one condition," he whispered.

"What's that?" Teagan's breathlessness made his heart pound harder.

He let the rush roll through him then teased her lips with his, not making contact, keeping them a breath apart. "That neither of us will be sorry."

"Promise." Teagan's fingers tightened against his chest. "I won't be."

CHAPTER NINE

TEAGAN PUSHED HER hands up his Henley, teasing her fingernails along the unbuttoned top of his collar. "Do you promise too?"

She asked in a way that was less about reassurance and more about urging him on. They didn't know what they were doing, but he was positive that wherever he went with her would be intense. "I promise."

His hands swept into her hair, brushing the thick strands back, and his lips tickled against hers, hovering a kiss away, living for each of her needy breaths. He erased the minute space, and Teagan's full lips stole his thoughts. Her hands drifted up, locking around his neck as he deepened their kiss, tongues testing, teasing—sliding with a growing want that consumed him.

Her soft sweater rubbed against him, and the curves of her breasts called for his attention. Teagan melted around his chest. His fingers threaded her hair, grabbing for more, holding onto the woman whose hot mouth opened and purred with a fiery fury.

They were gasping. Breathless. Her roaming hands explored his chest, knotting in his shirt, pulling Noah for more.

"Teagan…" He nibbled her lip then kissed her jawline, and the vibrations of her mews as her head dropped back were unlike any aphrodisiac he could recall.

This was a kiss. Nothing more. He needed to remember. Remind himself. Her hips rubbed against his growing erection, and Noah stifled a groan against her skin, biting and licking her earlobe until she moaned as he did.

She clung to his sides, her chest heaving against him when he whispered in her ear. Every word, each reaction, did nothing but urge him on, promising her the sweetest, most sinful things he could. Giving her the truth between the work his tongue levied from her ear to neck to lips.

I like how you sound.

I like how your kiss tastes.

That, Teagan, right there.

He pushed her until he couldn't take it anymore then pried his hands from her body and stapled them to the wall, on either side of her face.

"Your promise still good?" he asked.

Teagan nodded with cheeks that he had pinked and lips that were swollen from kissing him. "Still good."

"Me too." Noah pressed forward and softened his kisses, staring into the amber eyes that had darkened to a rich hazel.

Their wild, groping need eased to a silent watchful pause, waiting to see if they could survive a first kiss with explosive firepower.

Thump. Thump.

Teagan startled. Her gaze sobered. "What was that?"

He had an idea what that noise might've been. The thuds came from directly behind the wall.

Straightening her clothes, Teagan ducked under his arm, her face panicked.

"They're on the floor," Noah said quietly as Teagan walked into the living room.

He followed, and bingo. Bella and Will lay side by side

with their shared pillow in the middle. One of them had toppled, and having held each other, the other one fell.

"That could've been close," she mumbled, twisting toward him with wide eyes. "Maybe that was a bad idea."

His brow furrowed, and he had no idea what the hell to make of that. "Really?"

"I'm not sorry, but…" Teagan bit her lip. "What if they woke up? Or saw?"

He shrugged. "Then you explain."

"That I was making out with you in the hallway?" She rubbed her temples. "I just met you. What kind of example is that?"

Ouch. That was a first. Shot down and insulted. Was that twice in a row by the same woman in one night? Yeah, there was a record he wasn't thrilled to set.

She stared at the kids. "We didn't think that through."

"Right." He rolled his shoulders and stretched. "But we got it out of our system."

Teagan pivoted. "Maybe. Is that what we call that? Getting it out of our system?"

No. He'd call that a hot precursor to best-in-show sex. Nothing that happened in the hallway had gotten her out of his system. If anything, he'd had the taste he'd hoped for, and now he wanted more.

Teagan shook her head. "Can you imagine if Bella saw us?"

"She's a smart kid. Smarter than me half the time. I'd talk to her."

"If Bella got hurt again? I'd hate myself."

"Why would she get hurt?"

Teagan's hair fell to the side as her head tilted. "She thinks the world of you. Don't you know that?"

Flattery wasn't something he was comfortable with, and he

brushed it aside. "Same could be said for you too."

"She's special to me too, and she's lost her dad, her mom. If she saw us kiss and romanticized the idea…" Teagan pressed her lips together and lifted her shoulders. "It could break her little heart if it didn't go however she imagined."

Hell. When Teagan put it that way… Noah cringed. "Hadn't thought about it like that."

She bit her lip. "Now that you have?"

That was a lot of pressure to put on a kiss or even a friendship, which was what he wanted more than anything else from Teagan, even if it killed him to choose between touching her or simply being able to chill or ask questions if they came up. "Maybe we shouldn't have."

"You understand." Teagan wrapped her arms around him and hugged.

His eyes sank shut, and this was a gut punch. Clearly, Teagan hadn't been on the same page that said just being friends meant they couldn't touch. Noah breathed deep to ignore how she fit in his arm but then had to ignore how sweet she smelled. He grunted his answer, focusing on his platonic response more than any coherent agreement.

With an extra squeeze and a quiet thank-you, Teagan broke apart and headed to the couch. He followed, wondering what more he could add as she sat and twisted her leg underneath her. Noah took an overstuffed chair facing her. In his world, he'd always known what to say and how to say it. But in this new world, he wasn't the focus any more. *Hell*, this was his world now. He had to listen.

"What's that look?" she asked.

He dropped his head, staring at the carpet as heavy seconds drifted by before looking back at Teagan. "You have very intense eyes."

She blinked, sitting back as though that might change how powerful her gaze was. "That's a good thing?"

"They're sweet and true and just like everything about you." He inhaled slowly. "You're beautiful, and you're also so damn right."

Teagan's lips parted.

"I won't say that again, but I had to tonight. And one more thing."

She licked her bottom lip then quietly asked, "What?"

"In the hall." He blew out a slow breath of air. "That was intense, and that you put the brakes on because of them?" He nodded toward the floor. "You're really something special. A good mom, person in Bella's life—friend."

Teagan's cheeks pinked at the flattery, and he meant every word of it. "We're going to be good friends."

She stared at Will and Bella sleeping peacefully. "Despite the absurd number of times today that you proved I grossly misunderstood who you are. And I just met you."

A platonic friendship with Teagan could've meant death by slow torture, and maybe it was because he'd just experienced the hottest kiss of his life. But "I just met you" suddenly made him believe everything happened for a reason, and he'd have to sit back and figure out what that reason was.

CHAPTER TEN

"I'M READY." BELLA stood in front of her bedroom with a backpack on and the Velcro straps on her shoes fastened in place. "Uncle Noah." The little girl all but tsked. "You do not look ready."

That was because he wasn't. What were they ready for? School was over. He hadn't burned down the house in days. Heck, the weekend was so close he could taste it. But Noah seemed doomed for disaster, or at the very least disappointment, because whatever he was supposed to have done or gotten ready for, he hadn't even started.

His list of all things Bella-related had been left on his desk at Nuts and Bolts.

"Today's the day that I read to Gambler."

Gambler? Gambler! His buddy Zane's dog. How could he forget picking Bella up at the library a few months ago? Gambler was one canine that was hard to forget. A little bit crazy, a lot bit excitable, and unable to resist. Noah smiled, seeing that Bella was clearly under Gambler's charm as well, though he was clueless about the after-school activity.

"That's today?"

"Uh-huh." She nodded hard enough to make her glitter headband fall off.

"I have to be honest, ladybug." She wouldn't understand the level of mental exhaustion he was struggling with. "I didn't even have Gambler on my radar."

This week had kicked Noah's ass. Bella had morphed from his sweet niece to an unrecognizable tornado of a child after he purchased the wrong color of glitter hand sanitizer—no one had mentioned he should expect that. Then there was the drama of a monkey bar contest gone wrong, where Noah had choked down the urge to teach her how to elbow the little cheaters when no one was looking.

What he would've given for some pure physical exertion to drain him. He had dreams of BUD/S training where they dead lifted a telephone pole in the Pacific Ocean. He wanted to crawl to the top of a mountain with too much gear and not enough air. All of that sounded far easier than trying to figure out why she did, said, and ate nothing at school every day based on his after-school and dinnertime interrogations of her time spent at kindergarten. Though after checking in with her teacher, he found out that Bella was indeed doing, talking, and eating, and that he should ask different types of questions. Starting next week, he had a plan.

"How was lunch?" would become "How many bites of your sandwich did you eat?" Instead of "What did you do today?" he'd ask "What color markers did you color with?" Come Monday, Noah's tactics would be on point and ready to be deployed.

But right now he needed a strategy to achieve balance. Or sanity. How did moms manage everything? Bella barely had any activities outside of school, yet Noah's head was overloaded. There was a running list of birthday party invites, classroom volunteer opportunities, *appropriate* meal planning options...

"Okay. I won't practice reading aloud today." Her shoulders slumped. "I suppose I could read to you, though I excel when I read to Gambler."

Ugh. She was breaking out her SAT words on him and likely knew the definition of manipulation. "I think we have to RSVP for those things. Gambler might not even be there."

"He's always there. Gambler's daddy likes Miss Grace."

Noah cocked an eyebrow, thinking back to Teagan's concerns about how Bella might read things into adult relationships if she saw one forming. "Really? How do you know this?"

"They like each other." Bella took her backpack off. "What should I read to you?"

Noah's curiosity was suddenly stronger than his exhaustion. Would Zane know how Bella knew about him and Harper? Hell, what was Noah doing? Trying to see how much Bella could piece together about adults dating? That wouldn't change anything with him and Teagan. Still… "You're sure it's today?" He checked his watch, though he didn't know what time the program started.

"Yes, today. But we need to leave now. I have enough time to have a snack then drive without being rushed." She paused. "You can Google it if you want to check."

"I trust you." There was no point in double-checking the calendar, and he was struck by Lainey's words falling out of Bella's mouth. *Enough time to have a snack then drive without being rushed.* It sounded so like her. Never rushing. Always preparing for others, and that killed him. Everybody in Eagle's Ridge had had time to prepare for Lainey's death. Everyone except him.

Noah cleared his throat. "Sure thing. Let me go—"

Bella beamed. "I already packed my snack."

Of course, she did. She prepared like her mother. "Then let's load up."

Noah turned, and Bella skipped past him and pushed out the front door like the five-year-old that she was. All traces of her mom and the gifted, verbose child were gone. Either way, he was glad Bella was getting him out of the house. The fresh air and a new set of walls might do him some good.

★ ★ ★

"PLEASE, MOM. PLEASE. Please. Please. I never want to go. And now I want to go." Will pouted in the backseat as Teagan watched him in her rearview mirror.

She had a headache that wouldn't quit, and with school dismissing early today, she hadn't finished everything that she needed to. Will dropping a library bomb on her shouldn't have been a problem. But his complete overreaction to her balking *was*.

Not that she wanted to punish him for wanting to read, but Teagan wondered why it had to be today. Oh, what the heck. How often did Will beg to go to the library? Never. "Only…"

"Thank you!" he chimed with a quick kick of his legs.

"Only because we love books and we love libraries, but we do not love attitude problems. Do you read me?" She flicked a glance at the rearview mirror, and he beamed.

"I read you!"

If anyone ever said that advisors had kids figured out, they were nuts. Teagan changed course and maneuvered through town, easing down the quiet tree-lined street, then pulled into the parking lot.

She gave another glance into her backseat. She had never seen him this ready to be at the library before, and as soon as she shifted into Park, Will fumbled with his belt. She unbuckled her own seat belt, and he was out the door, barely slamming it hard enough for it to click before he rushed toward the library.

The quaint library was one story and wrapped with a thick line of old trees shading its expansive porch. Teagan loved its bright red doors, but Will beelined away from the entrance.

"What on earth?" She didn't see where he was—or why he didn't go inside—and Teagan snagged her purse from the passenger seat then swiftly trailed him. "Will?"

The parking lot was filled, but that wasn't a surprise. It was a busy place, but there was nothing to indicate what had caught his interest. Her heart pounded. He wasn't one to take off, and truthfully, he was a bit tenderhearted. If he was ever separated or lost, he'd worry.

Teagan rushed around the corner, no longer able to see her son. Until she did. His little feet had carried him across a small field to a group of kids and dogs nestled on blankets.

This was the program where kids read to animals. Teagan took a relieved breath and pushed her sunglasses into her hair, getting a better look at the faces. Certainly, Will had sat with Bella. Then a quiet laugh startled her from behind.

She spun and saw two men. "Noah? And... Zane?"

Teagan had met the other man at a fundraising race, and she'd seen him around town lately with Harper Grace, the librarian.

Zane gave a quick wave. "Nice to see you, Teagan. I was just catching up with my old friend."

"Don't let me interrupt you. I was"—she gestured toward the group—"catching up with my kid."

Both men cracked smiles, but Zane begged off. "I need to keep an eye on Gambler. He's fine until a rabbit hops by. Then..." He shook his head. "Pandemonium. Gets the kids laughing, though."

The men shook hands goodbye, and Noah eased onto a bench. He had an arm thrown over the back, and he tossed a lazy wave for her to come closer. "You can join me if you like."

"I didn't expect to see you."

"I could tell. I'm not sure you expected to see anyone." He tapped the empty space to his side. "And you look confused, which is my look, considering Bella spent thirty minutes explaining a toy she hopes Santa brings her."

Teagan stepped closer. "Why's that confusing?"

"Because the things are named after text speak or emojis. The entire time I thought she was trying to sound like a big kid." The corners of his mouth curved and his lips pinched as though he knew how ridiculous the situation sounded. "I was translating in my head. Laugh out loud. Be right back, or something. I don't know, but it turns out that's what these things are called."

"You win the day." Teagan slapped a hand over her mouth and still giggled. "Oh, man."

"Like she's getting a smiling pile of poop." Noah scowled. "How about these two letters—N. O."

Teagan couldn't find him any more endearing. "Okay, you've got to let it go. Emojis aren't going anywhere." She leaned closer and whispered, "But you don't have to buy smiling piles of anything."

"Fair enough." He half grinned. "Tell me a funny story from your day."

"I had a kid in fourth grade sent to my office today about a money tree."

His brow pinched. "What's a money tree? Other than, man, I wish I had a money tree."

"Close." She tilted her head. "Apparently, if you nag your

mom long enough for something, she will shake the money tree and it will arrive."

"What?"

Teagan nodded. "Yeah. Needless to say, I have a kicking headache."

"And how was this your problem?"

"His science teacher wasn't making progress, talked to the parents, who wouldn't correct their kid, who doesn't believe in Santa, but does believe in the money tree." Teagan rubbed her temples. "Maybe one of my top ten most-interesting-and-frustrating parent-teacher-child conferences ever."

"You don't get paid enough." He pursed his lips, failing to hide his laughter. "Whatever you make, that's not enough."

"I don't know how we ended up here. I just wanted a little quiet." She finally perched on the edge of the bench, putting far too much thought into how far—or close—she should sit. "We've never been to this program before."

"Me, either."

Teagan laughed and massaged the headache at the base of her neck. The fresh air and good company would help.

"There's a pressure point that might help. If that's a tension headache." He pointed below and then in between his eyebrows. "Take two fingers, like this. Press for a minute then give it a break. You can also do the base of your skull and neck."

"Really? Thanks. I rarely get headaches."

He shrugged. "It's handy to know if you're in the middle of nowhere and one pops up."

Wow, he could play down his heroics. She switched to her neck. "Middle of nowhere with a headache, huh?"

"No, try more like..." Noah scooted over, brushing her hair away. His hands covered hers, holding her fingers still and pressing her thumbs deeper. "Do you feel that?"

"Maybe." The reaction sparkling through her was more about his touch than headache mitigation, and she didn't want him to think she was so shallow a touch could make her flustered. "I think so, thanks."

"No, that's not it, then." He brushed her hands away. "You would know."

Noah ran his hands down her shoulder, twisting her on the bench to position her for better access, then he put his hands on her neck again. They were warm and still. Strong. His thumbs pressed the top of her hairline then slid down her spinal column. Teagan's insides fluttered, same as before when his hands covered hers, then he stilled again. The pads of his thumbs moved away from her spine with a steady pressure until he stopped again.

"Right here," he said, kneading her neck then increasing the strength of his touch with a steady push.

Her head dipped back, and Teagan's breath left as her eyes fluttered shut. A rush of bliss made her mouth taste sweet, and she inhaled deeply, rolling her head up as he carefully released her neck.

"Like that." Noah kept a hand at the back of her head.

Teagan took account of her body. The headache had dulled significantly. Was it even there? But better, her muscles had relaxed. She eased to face him again, not wanting to break the trance he'd cast over her loose muscles. "How did you do that?"

"Pressure points." He shrugged.

"Magic."

"In martial arts, you can use pressure points to immobilize a person, right?"

She nodded.

"Same concept. Pressure points can be applied to basic human reactions. Pain, pleasure. It opens or closes blood flow, releases natural chemicals that can hurt or heal." Noah didn't scoot back, and their chemistry didn't care what barriers they'd erected after they'd kissed. The connection was still there. "All useful things to have in the field if you can't pop ibuprofen for a headache."

Her headache had gone, but her interest in his hands had not. "That really helped."

This was the awkward moment, those few minutes that would define whether they could really be friends, and Teagan didn't want to lose him. She couldn't. Noah had an indescribable quality that made her smile in a way that she hadn't smiled all day. Shifting her purse into her lap, she brought their attention back to the kids. "Will isn't at Bella's reading level. I'm surprised he knew about this."

Noah watched her a second longer than was comfortable and eased back against the bench, not sliding away, and cast a long glance onto the field. "She's been doing this for a few months now. Maybe they talked about it."

Maybe they did, but that was a lot of excitement coming from her backseat for a passing mention. How else would Will know where to go? "Do you think…"

What if the kids had planned their get-together? But that was a stretch. Wasn't it? Had Bella seen something? Or heard? Were they really asleep the other night? Teagan's mind began to race, and she worried that she and Noah had already messed up. Even now, did friends share pressure points? Her cheeks flamed.

"Do I think what?" he asked.

"Nothing." Teagan batted away her crazy idea. They successfully handled a post-kiss meetup where they had touched, but it didn't seem awkward now. That was a huge success! They were friends! She couldn't ask for anything more.

The wind picked up fall leaves, and they watched the kids read to animals, occasionally straying to roll away and blow dandelions seeds then rush back to their blankets and dogs.

Noah turned, tilting his head. "What do you think they're doing?"

"Blowing the dandelions?" She turned back to Noah. "Didn't you do that when you were a kid?"

"Create a weed problem for my parents?"

"No!" She rolled her eyes. "They're making wishes!"

"Oh, right." He quieted. "Lainey used to do that."

How was he handling losing Lainey? Was he a talker or someone who bottled up tighter if asked? "Are you okay?"

Noah lifted a thick shoulder. "Not really."

"That was unexpectedly honest."

His smile cracked, and he turned, seemingly amused. "That's me."

"So I'm learning. A SEAL with a soft side."

"Whoa, hey now." He tossed his hands in the air but winked. "I wouldn't go that far." After he dropped his hands and the joking subsided, he shrugged. "That's life. Maybe that's what they're out there wishing for. A great life."

"A fairy-tale happily ever after."

He studied the kids for a second longer. "Yeah, maybe. Who wouldn't want that?"

Teagan watched him relax. Even if she couldn't read his mind, it looked as though it was the first time Noah wasn't worried about raising Bella. "I'm happy you're back in Eagle's Ridge."

And she bit her tongue to keep from admitting how glad she was to sit next to him too.

CHAPTER ELEVEN

T HE WIND PICKED up, howling. The cloudy day had been scattered with storms, but the worst of the weather had passed. Teagan nestled under an afghan on her couch with a pile of notes from the third-grade homerooms. She reached for her mug that had the bright red block print I'M NOT JUDGING YOU, the more delicate script underneath reading I'M PROFESSIONALLY DIAGNOSING YOU, and took a long sip of the decaf mint tea.

Maybe she should've opted for the taller mug that rah-rahed her when she was on a roll with teacher notes. She could quote her favorite mug and made a point to bring it to certain meetings with parents or teachers on the off chance they'd read her mug and have an epiphany.

BEHIND EVERY *JUST KIDDING*—There's the truth.

PEEKING AROUND THE *I DON'T CARES*—There's a hope or a hurt.

WITH EVERY *I DON'T KNOW*—There's an idea wanting to shine.

Heck, if Teagan had the funding, she'd gift all the teachers in her school with that mug. She spun her pen on her fingers, wondering what she would do for the holidays, and the wind blew again, louder than it had been gusting. Today's storm was over, but the wind hadn't left.

Crack.

Teagan startled, spilling mint tea on the stack of papers, and quickly shook the papers dry. There it was again. It wasn't distant thunder or lightning striking close by, more like a snap or a crack but muffled, and she had no idea what it was.

Teagan put down the tea-dampened papers and listened to the hum of her central heat. Nothing else made a peep. Not even the wind. Whatever that had been, it seemed out of place after a day of branches shaking and wind howling.

She tossed her pen onto the coffee table, next to her mug and papers, and again listened until the blood whirled in her eardrums. Still nothing. Maybe she shouldn't have watched a Halloween cartoon marathon with Will. The cartoons weren't scary at the time. *But look at me now.*

Teagan smiled at how easily Will had gone to sleep hours ago. Maybe she needed to go to bed herself.

Crack.

"What is that?" The hairs on the back of her neck stood, and she unwrapped from her cozy afghan at the speed of a snail. "Okay. Let's figure this out."

She crept along her living room, killing the only light, then checked her front door and back. Both were locked. Still no more weird noises. It was just the wind, and she needed to relax. There were a million new noisemaking possibilities with all the new Halloween decorations, a zombie or a ghost smacking a garage, or a fake graveyard or a banshee scratching a fence.

But those wouldn't make a cracking noise that seemed to come from her backyard. "Goblins and ghosts, oh my." She grumbled to herself.

She leaned against the counter to peek out the window.

Again, nothing. Only a black abyss.

Her paranoia compounded, and when she looked down, the phone patiently waited with a blinking notification. She swiped the screen. She had missed a text message from Noah, and Teagan opened it.

NOAH: *Are you awake? Probably not. It's late.*

She picked up the phone, not bothering to text back, and hit Call. What would she say? At this point, her nerves were so jumbled it didn't matter.

"Hey, Teagan?" He answered quickly. "I hope I didn't wake you."

"You're not in my backyard, are you?" She cringed. That didn't sound right. Or sane.

"Uh, no." He cleared his throat. "Are you okay?"

"Ha." She put her hand to her temple as the flames of embarrassment flared. "Never mind. That was ridiculous to ask."

"By the tone of your voice, you didn't think so a minute ago."

A minute ago, she hadn't heard herself speak. He had to think she was losing it. Heck, right now maybe she was. Just the other day, she had sworn she saw somebody walking around the backyard, but when she went to check, no one was there.

"I'm fine. If someone was going to break in, they wouldn't make so much noise, and they wouldn't draw out the process."

"What are you talking about?"

"'Tis the season for creepy thoughts, I guess." Still she couldn't sit down, and wandering back to the living room, Teagan wrapped the afghan back around her and sat upright in the center of her couch, listening for any noise that might sound like that cracking, stripping, plastic-breaking crack that had caught her off guard. "I'm going to go to bed. I think I've seen too many scary movies. I'm sorry to bother you, Noah."

"Do you want me to swing by and check things out?" he asked.

Wouldn't that be nice? She hesitated. But what was he going to do, load Bella into his truck? Teagan drew a deep breath and picked up her tea. "That's not necessary, but I appreciate the offer." She took a slow sip. "I'm gonna put myself to bed now."

"You still sound concerned."

Teagan bit her lip. "Well, I was. But now I'm just going to say sweet dreams."

There were very few times that Teagan wished she had another person to curl up next to in bed. She wasn't someone who liked to be held when she slept. The idea of cuddling and spooning worked in the books, but to each his own. It wasn't just that she was an independent person, it was that she liked to have her own space. Tonight, though, having Noah to lean against would've been nice. Even if she had rolled away to take her own space later.

"All right, then. Sweet dreams, Teagan."

The call ended, leaving her with her phone limp in her hand.

That was a red flag that she should have seen with her ex-husband. Teagan never wanted to be next to him when they were lying in bed. She liked touching him when it was mutually beneficial, but afterward? She'd never been interested.

She'd always assumed it was because of her independent and strong personality. But maybe not so much. Was she any less strong for calling Noah tonight and wanting to cuddle with him now?

No, she didn't think so. He didn't present as the stereotypical alpha male, oozing dominance but in a respectful way.

Like a partner.

That was something to think about. Tomorrow. After she had enough sleep so that the outdoors didn't make her jump when it snapped, crackled, and popped.

★   ★   ★

THAT DIDN'T SIT right. Noah tossed his cell phone back and forth then rolled up in bed. Not two minutes beforehand, his mind had been cloudy, but now he was firing on all cylinders and unsure what to do about it.

Bella was tucked in bed, and calling Teagan back to double-check felt like the wrong thing to do.

"Are you in my backyard?" What kind of question was that? The kind that he wasn't comfortable with.

He paced from the guest bedroom where he had been sleeping to the master bedroom, which slowly was becoming useful again, and stood in front of the chest of drawers where he'd finally unpacked his clothes.

Even if he got dressed, what was he going to do? Nothing. Bella was asleep, and even if she wasn't, he couldn't take her to a situation where Teagan was scared.

Or was she? Was he searching for someone to save because the career he had loved was gone?

No, this wasn't a chance to play hero for the girl he had a crush on. His instincts had never been adrenaline driven, and he'd never gone in search of accolades. Something was wrong, and he quickly dressed in street clothes.

He didn't want to call his folks. It was too late, and they'd have too many questions. The guys that he'd reconnected with?

What if Bella woke up? She'd met Zane in passing because of Gambler, but Wyatt had done a few solid favors for him and Lainey before he got home.

Noah scrolled through his phone contacts and swiped his buddy's name. It rang three times before a groggy Wyatt answered.

"Hello?"

"Hey, man. It's Noah, and I know it's late. But is there any way you can run over here? I'd love it if you could watch Bella."

"Everything okay?" Wyatt asked, yawning.

Noah ran a hand over the scruff on his chin. "Wyatt, man. I know you're good at your job, and you'll get me when I say I don't know."

The voice cleared on the other side. "See you in ten."

CHAPTER TWELVE

HEADLIGHTS ROLLED INTO Noah's driveway as he paced by the front door. The panic in Teagan's voice was seared into Noah's memory despite her protests that nothing was wrong. If nothing was wrong, she wouldn't have called. Or she might have, but that wasn't what she'd say.

Wyatt jogged to the front door, and Noah let him in.

"Bella's asleep. She shouldn't wake up."

His friend eyed the concealed carry tucked under Noah's shirt at his waist. "If you want me to go with you, Paige can come over here instead."

Noah shook his head. "It's probably nothing."

"I can't believe it's nothing if you're locked and loaded."

"True enough." Noah's fingers curled by his sides, and he was itching to bolt out the door. He gave a curt nod. "I'll explain when I get back."

Wyatt's jaw set as he lifted his chin in measured deliberation. "All right, partner. Stay safe."

If Noah'd had any parting promises to offer, he'd have done so. But his only response was to hustle out the door and hope that he was overreacting. Everything was fine. An animal got into her trash. A branch cracked. The storms had loosened a wood plank. He continued making the list as he revved his truck and headed toward Teagan's.

Of course, all this could be overreacting. She hadn't asked

him to come over. Was this too much? He rubbed his chest as he made a tight turn, hauling double the residential speed limit.

If nothing was wrong and she knew he came over anyway, he might need to reassess his gut instincts. But they were never wrong.

"You're not in my backyard, are you?"

Noah made the final turn toward her street and pulled over a block short of her house then slid out of his truck. He gently pressed his door shut.

The night was eerily calm with the now familiar cool Northwest fall weather, and Noah bypassed the obvious path, the sidewalk, and skipped into the neighbor's backyard.

Not even a dog barked. His senses were set on high, and his eyes had adjusted to the evening. He could see among the trees and the shadows. He searched for anything out of place, coming up empty.

"What's bothering you?" he whispered, walking down the fence line near the back of Teagan's house until he scaled her low fence.

The house lights were off and the window shades drawn. There was nothing back here except for a soccer ball, an oversized shed, and a well-kept lawn.

This wasn't normal. He'd crossed the line from protective friend to… Who knew what to call this? But there was nothing here, and her lights were out, so clearly she wasn't worried anymore.

Still, his senses tingled, and he made a sweep. Everything was as he had seen it before. Trash cans where he expected them to be. Tree branches barely rustling with a breeze.

Noah walked the way he came, admitting defeat and feeling paranoid.

Did he miss the action and adventure more than he knew? Was he going mad from denying himself the one woman who made sense? White spots reflecting on the ground broke his attention at the corner of the house, and he dropped his gaze.

His senses fired alarms. His hand hovered on the ready as he changed course, sliding closer to the house, near a window, to inspect. Cigarette butts, several of them, piled outside a window.

Someone had been by her house for an extended period. Doing what? And when?

Just because she heard a noise didn't mean it happened tonight, but he hated coincidences. Noah scanned the backyard then searched the front.

What was he supposed to do with a pile of old smoke butts? Wake her up and scare the pants off her? He made another pass and decided to head home, not waking and scaring Teagan. There wasn't anyone here... At least that he could see.

CHAPTER THIRTEEN

THE CALM NIGHT did nothing to settle Noah as he patrolled the quiet neighborhood, listening to the steady breeze, and found zip. He needed to go home and explain to Wyatt where he had gone so late at night. But for now, Noah didn't care about his opinion. A boulder of worry still lodged in his chest, and he couldn't shake Teagan's tone of voice. There were simple answers to a pile of cigarette butts. A landscaper who ate lunch in the same place and didn't clean up his smokes. Or a... Actually, Noah had no other readily available excuses.

But he was going to have to admit to creeping in her backyard. Otherwise, he was nothing more than a creep.

Opting to take the sidewalk instead of her neighbor's backyard, Noah pulled out his cell phone.

NOAH: *When you have a free sec tomorrow, let me know.*

Noah shoved his phone back into his pocket, passing a man as he headed back to his dually truck. Despite the man's clean-cut clothes and windbreaker, an uneasy feeling stirred inside Noah as they passed. A dog walker would make sense. But someone out for a stroll at this hour? Unease prickled—

"Excuse me," the unknown man called, breaking Noah's thoughts.

Surprised but not caught off guard, Noah slowly pivoted,

his defenses up, and strode closer. "Yeah. Can I help you?"

"Actually, I was wondering the same thing about you."

Noah's eyes narrowed. "I'm sorry?"

"I keep an eye on the neighborhood and don't recognize you."

Noah didn't know whether to chuckle in solidarity with the lone watchman or question who was roaming the streets as a vigilante huntsman. "I'm just visiting a friend. But good looking out, man."

"What friend?"

Defensive, Noah took a step closer. "And who are you?"

"Whose friend are you?" the man pushed.

The telltale prickles that the situation was not what it seemed stood up at the base of Noah's neck. "How about we start with your name?"

The guy was a block away from Teagan's house after her hearing weird noises. Noah was on high alert.

"Edward Lee."

Noah's gut said that Edward Lee was a made-up name, but he had friends at a black ops firm who could quickly run his background check. "The neighborhood watch takes themselves seriously around here, don't they?"

"Can never be too careful about who is near our most valuable possessions."

He scoffed. "What's that? Cars and boats?"

"Family, of course."

"Of course..." Noah followed up. "Who do you work with over at Eagle's Ridge PD? I have some buddies and would love to do this in my neighborhood."

"Did I get your name?" Edward asked.

"No, you didn't."

They sized one another up.

"Noah Coleman."

There was no shaking hands. No pleasant follow-up. Only suspicion both ways.

Noah thought of one quick test. "I've gotta roll." He turned to leave then eased back. "Hey, do you have any smokes? I left my cigarettes back at my friends', and I don't think anywhere in town is open."

Edward's hands shoved deep into his pockets as he rolled back on his heels. "Don't smoke. Can't help you." Then he turned and left without another word.

Noah watched the guy disappear then headed to his truck and climbed in. After a long moment reflecting on how deep a hole he was digging, Noah swiped the screen and pulled up his contacts, pausing as his thumb hovered over two hacker names. Both would be able to pull the same information, but one had more official means while the other knew where to check the shadows for secrets. He pressed Call but was sent straight to voicemail. The tone beeped for a message. "Hey, Lexi, this is Noah Coleman. I'm calling for a favor, and I know I'll owe you. But if you could let me know anything on an Edward Lee from Eagle's Ridge, Washington, I'd love to see it."

He left his contact information, hung up, and rubbed his hands on his face. He'd called Wyatt and now Lexi, and all because his gut said Teagan wasn't telling him something. Maybe Noah needed to take a look at himself and not everyone else because if he was off base, he'd really messed up.

IT TOOK FIVE minutes to drive home, and he parked in the driveway before slipping through the door quietly to find Wyatt playing on his phone.

"Are you going to tell me what's going on now? Wyatt

tossed the cell down. "Because I have a solid reputation I like to hold on to." He gestured between them. "Past or no past, we're not talking about transgressions that'll land us in detention like back in high school."

Noah unholstered his weapon, heading for the gun safe in his bedroom. "Give me a minute."

Wyatt narrowed his eyes, giving Noah hell. "Not like I don't have a warm bed and beautiful woman to go home to."

They were joking. He knew it, but his grin was forced, and that pang in his chest was uncomfortable. He didn't know what to call it. Jealousy, envy ... that was all wrong because he was happy for Wyatt. "You're lucky to have her awake and waiting."

"Even if she's not." Wyatt settled against the couch, back to playing the game on his phone again. "I'm a lucky bastard."

Noah's chest lifted with silent but heartfelt appreciation of his old friend's sentiments as he went to stow his gun. With a quick finger combo and a thumb scan, the safe popped open, and he'd safely disarmed and returned to the living room. Wyatt tossed the phone again then checked his watch. "You have two minutes and counting to explain why you didn't find what you went looking for, but you're still concerned."

"Not bad, big shot."

There was a reason Wyatt was trusted in his field. The man's eyes missed nothing, even as he kicked back.

Noah shook his head, joined Wyatt on the couch, then looked at his friend, wanting to share without coming off as though he was cracking up after leaving the military and looking for problems to fix. As best he could, he gave a sixty-second rundown including Teagan's phone call, the neighborhood canvass, the pile of cigarettes, and the neighborhood watchman with his hands in his pockets.

Wyatt shook his head. "If he weren't off exploring the wild

blue yonder, I'd say I never trusted the ex-husband."

"Did you know him?" Noah glanced at him from the corner of his eyes, not expecting to hear that.

"Nope. Just heard whispers of him. I've made it my business to know a little bit about everyone."

Noah snorted. That was Wyatt, the lone protector, always quiet and observing. But Noah frowned, uncertain why Teagan's ex would spy on her. "I didn't think the ex was hung up on Teagan when they split."

"It doesn't have to work that way."

"Meaning what?" Noah asked.

"Spencer doesn't have to care to see her as his," Wyatt explained. "And this town? Why come back when everyone knows it's not for his family."

"She doesn't think they know."

"Why does a guy like that ever marry a woman like her in a town like Eagle's Ridge?" Wyatt lifted a shoulder. "It stands out."

Noah could list a hundred reasons why any sane male would marry Teagan. Her heart, her smile, how she cared.

"She'd be amazing to be with," Noah volunteered.

Wyatt shook his head. "There's a difference between hanging with a woman and planning for the future."

"Makes sense." An emptiness hit Noah as he dropped his head back on the couch. He wasn't envious that Wyatt had a woman to crawl in bed with, but he wished he had Teagan to hold. To plan with—maybe for the future? Definitely more than for a few days and beyond a warm bed and ensuing hot night. Though that would be a bonus Noah wouldn't complain about. Just like Wyatt, Noah would call himself a lucky man if he was within a shooting chance of that kind of future.

He rubbed his chest, concentrating on the night's troubles

and not the unsettled hollow feeling eating at him. "I'm too close to see what you can."

"What makes you think I do?" Wyatt asked.

"Because I know your perspective. It doesn't matter that we grew up on different sides of the river or that it's been this many years since high school detention."

Wyatt nodded and quietly laughed.

"We might've been on different SEAL teams, but once a SEAL, always a SEAL." Noah rubbed his temples. "You're not going to give me a BS answer when I need a heads-up."

"I don't trust a man who has no reason to stay and never quite leaves." Wyatt shrugged. "But it makes more sense that you stopped an angry kid, a PTA member gone nuts, or a would-be thief from running off with an armful of counseling files."

Noah's brow pinched. He tried to picture anyone at school that upset with the woman who had recently worn a black sweater with two white stick figures on it. One held a line above its head, the other was missing the line body, and the text said, "I'm a school counselor. I've got your back."

Wyatt shifted on the couch. "Teagan has dirt on half the families in this town—stuff that Hildie could only dream of and hormone-crazed teenagers would go nuts for."

Noah couldn't imagine. All things he hadn't considered. "Hmm."

"How about this?" Wyatt stood. "I'll make a call to a detective friend and see what he thinks, then I'll follow up with you in the morning."

Noah could get behind that plan. "Okay. That works for me."

"Now if you'll excuse me, I'm headed to bed."

Lucky bastard.

CHAPTER FOURTEEN

ONE FOLLOW-UP PHONE call with Wyatt and Noah found himself heading to the Eagle's Ridge Police Department with a detective's name on a Post-It Note instead of heading straight into Nuts and Bolts. The office was small and quiet, and the detective was awaiting him.

By the time Noah was shown to the officer's desk, he was certain that everyone had mentioned he was the one who'd burned down Lainey's house. *To the ground.*

"Wyatt is your friend." The detective leaned back in the scarred office chair and rolled a toothpick between his fingers. "We did him a favor."

Noah worked his jaw back and forth. "I appreciate that. He also mentioned that I need to speak with you. Meaning, we're all friends."

"You put me in a predicament."

The meeting wasn't off to a great start. "That wasn't my intention. I had a concern, and if it was unfounded, I didn't want to needlessly worry Teagan."

The detective popped the toothpick into his mouth, holding it between his teeth like a plank before he relaxed and worked the side of his gum. "And what's your relationship with Miss Shaw?"

Good question. "What's that have to do with this?"

He lifted a shoulder. "You're new in town, question suspicious activity, and that's not something we're used to."

Man, did Noah hate the new-in-town line. He wasn't one to name-drop, just as he didn't use his service in the military as a shiny object to get attention. But he was raised in Eagle's Ridge and born in a hospital that bore his family name—the Coleman Center.

"I wouldn't say I'm new to town. 'Returning' might be a better word."

The toothpick worked its way to the other side of the detective's mouth. "Ah."

This was a waste of time. Noah would have better luck getting secondhand information from Wyatt. "All right, thank you for your time, detective." Noah stood, ready to shake his hand and get to work. Not that there were cars in line for tune-ups yet, but if he didn't at least show up, there never would be.

"The cigarette butts." The detective motioned for him to remain seated.

Noah rolled his shoulders but dropped into the chair. "What about them?"

"They could've been piled up in the corner by someone who works there on a regular basis. A cleaning service not allowed to smoke inside. A landscaper, a next-door neighbor kid sneaking off to grab a smoke."

He lifted his chin. "All things I've considered, which is why I talked to Wyatt."

"But they were fresh butts. Smoked about the same time."

Noah raised his brows and rolled his bottom lip into his mouth and thought. "Hmm."

"*Hmm* is right." He shifted the toothpick. "Why were you over there?"

Surely Wyatt had already shared, but Noah was sure that this was something the detective had to ask, anyway.

Noah filled the man in on his conversation with Teagan and how he planned to explain everything that had gone on thus far but had not yet done so. The detective nodded then pulled out the toothpick and rolled it between his fingers.

"Look, but those cigarette butts, that's concerning," the detective said. "But it's the positioning that concerns me. Not just the window but the corner of the house, with a view of the driveway and the neighbor."

"What? Like a lookout?" Noah's brow pinched.

The detective rocked in his office chair. "I took a gander around the back side of her property. She doesn't keep her shed locked."

"Who locks their shed?" Noah shrugged. "I have no idea."

"It's insulated. Expensive, not the run-of-the-mill kind that you can order online and assemble from a prefab kit. You don't buy those at hardware stores. It was built some time ago."

"Okay," Noah said, failing to understand where the conversation was going.

"The insulation had been stripped out, which is odd. But it doesn't look like it's used often. Could've been an animal, could've been long ago."

Noah leaned forward, resting his forearms on the detective's desk. "Was it?"

"Nope." He shook his head. "That wasn't an animal. But as for when? No idea."

Why would someone open the shed walls? "Anything else you can tell me?"

The detective shook his head. "There's nothing to share. Hell, it's not even an investigation. She hasn't called in a concern or a crime. This was nothing more than a friend of mine asking about a concern for his friend. I looked, and we talked."

Noah ran his hand over his chin. "I get it. And I really appreciate it."

"If you talk to Teagan, and she's concerned, have her file a police report. Otherwise…" The detective shrugged then tossed his toothpick into the trash can.

Otherwise, Noah realized, this was just a weird occurrence, brought on by a noise that she had heard during a week of storms. The cigarettes were weird but not criminal. Still, they were suspicious enough that he would be on alert. Noah stood up and extended his hand. "Thanks again for your time."

"I'll have someone drive her street every now and then."

"Appreciate that." And now Noah had the awkward task of explaining to Teagan that he'd scoped her backyard without letting her know and confided in an old friend, who then sent the police to do the same.

All in all, Noah should have looped her into the conversation much earlier. It was too late for that, and he had nothing much to share other than his boundary crossing and a strange pile of cigarettes.

CHAPTER FIFTEEN

EVERY STATION ON the radio irritated Noah. Commercials seemed trivial, radio hosts annoying, and too many songs had lyrics that spoke to him. He read between the lines and heard about the trust that Lainey had bestowed upon him by letting him raise Bella, the same trust that he might've overstepped by going to Teagan's at night. Noah's angst left him confused over his protective nature and how he wanted to protect Teagan specifically.

He flipped off the radio and concentrated on the list of action items for Nuts and Bolts. His CPA had sent him a list of accounts payable items he needed to categorize. He hoped for a customer or two to drop by but guessed that wouldn't happen until the afternoon.

The truck's tires ate the road as he wound his way through Eagle's Ridge. Noah drummed his thumbs on the steering wheel, uncomfortable in the silence and his worries that kept going back to Teagan.

He couldn't be alone with his thoughts right now, and hell, what did it matter if he was on time to the shop? With a quick change of lanes, Noah pulled a left-hand turn and headed to see if Adam or Zane were around at A To Z Watersports.

As soon as he had a plan, Noah relaxed, and by the time he parked and jumped from his dually, he was in a better place.

He wandered up to the watersports business in what appeared to be a large old house. The front door had a sign that read "Come On In."

He pulled the door handle open and let himself inside. "Hello?" Noah stepped in. "Zane? Adam?"

"Hey, man, what are you doing here?" Adam came from the right, off the edge of a desk he'd perched on, and tossed his clipboard down.

Noah marveled at how a space that had likely been a sitting room in this large house seemed perfect as a reception area. "Stopping in to see how the place looks."

Adam proudly gestured to the renovated room, and Noah nodded his approval as he listened to the quiet bluegrass playing in the background.

A To Z was comforting and homey. Actually, it reminded him of his parents' house with its beloved wood detailing and always-brewing coffee. Familiar thoughts from his past tugged at his heartstrings until he couldn't help being reminded of Lainey.

Noah remembered how he and Lainey would go to No Man's Land after the Founders' Day celebrations and order HALO pancakes drowned in whipped cream and a syrup that they called rocket fuel. Hell, it was hard to believe so many years had gone by and that they'd lost touch then reconnected.

When Adam and Zane had come to Noah's house on his first day back in Eagle's Ridge, they didn't reference the last time he was in town—for Lainey's funeral. Nor had they relived the painful conversation where Noah broke the news about Lainey over beers at Baldie's.

Why those memories rushed at him now, Noah had no idea, especially when his visit to A To Z was about escaping Lainey. Except, he wasn't trying to escape. He simply needed a conversation that wasn't built around life's worries and downsides.

Noah backed out of the reception area and let out a low whistle. "This place is impressive."

"Appreciate that." Adam walked in step with Noah.

"I meant to tell you that it's really something how you've opened this for tours and rentals." Noah admired the work the brothers had done.

"There's also the boat house and an apartment."

"Sounds big." The place seemed as though it would continue to unfold if he turned corner after corner. "Do you live there?"

Adam shook his head. "No. Jane and I are building a place."

He lifted his chin upon hearing of the major step in Adam and Jane's relationship, but he still couldn't believe that someone wouldn't wake up to the possibilities of this place. "I won't say too bad, but man, someone should live here."

"We had camps here all summer."

"Yeah?" Noah smiled at the vision of kids and laughter filling the house and the surrounding forest and water. He could send Bella to camps when she was old enough. What kind of camps would she like? He'd loved sports camps. Did they have other types? Like gifted program or reading camps? And how life had changed that those thoughts even popped into his head now. He rubbed his chin as that sank in.

"It's an adventure camp for at-risk youth," Adam added.

Noah nodded. "Solid."

"But I know you didn't stop by just to check out the place. What can I do you for?" Adam thumbed over his shoulder. "We got a rad new surfskis that just came in. Fiberglass and carbon mix. Closed deck, thirty-seven pounds. No one's even seen it if you want first dibs."

Noah laughed. "What the heck is a surfski?"

"They don't train you SEALs in the latest state-of-the-art equipment?" Adam walked on back, and Noah followed him to a room where equipment was stacked and stored. "This beauty"—he waved his hand over a slender canoe—"is a surfski."

Noah admired the narrow kayak but still side-eyed his friend. "Yeah, I don't know about that word."

Adam walked along the side and let his fingers trace the shock cord deck rigging. "Don't knock the power of the surfskis. It's like a kayak but lighter. Very narrow, and rounded, so maybe your big, clumsy ass should stick to a kayak. We don't need to have you tipping out on the river."

"Yeah, right." Noah scoffed as if he wouldn't hit the water, but this thing was nothing more than an overgrown drinking straw. Balancing would take a hot second. He moved toward the hull and angled down to get a good look at the cockpit and seat.

"It's like balancing on a log. Only the best survive. Maybe you should stick to something like whitewater rafting." Adam held his arms out as if balancing on a tight rope. "More room to spread out."

"Sounds like a challenge." Noah straightened and let his hand drift along the edge, resting on the carrying grip. "Sign me up for the all-powerful surfski."

They laughed, and it felt good to bullshit and joke with Adam. All they needed was for Zane and Gambler to walk in, and he could practically see the future of his life in Eagle's Ridge rekindling without the catalyst of a major event. No one had died. No huge life changes were imminent. Just two old friends catching up as though it hadn't been too long. But his stopping by wasn't entirely without purpose, and now that he was here, he could talk to Adam about Nuts and Bolts.

"But not today, though." Noah paced the length of the room and turned.

"Fair enough."

"You have a few minutes to talk?" Though if he asked about Teagan, he'd be overstepping. Again.

"Of course." Adam crossed his arms and leaned against a metal pole.

"Teagan."

Adam's brows arched. "Unexpected turn in the conversation."

"Tell me about it." Noah ran a hand over his face. "Look, you've known her for a while?"

"Since she moved to Eagle's Ridge. I'm not sure when. But she's always been involved in the community. A bit outdoorsy."

"Did you know her ex?"

"Yeah, sure. Spencer comes in town every now and then, stocks up on equipment sometimes." Adam rolled his eyes. "The guy's a"—he made air quotes—"treasure hunter, whatever that means."

"Is he…" Noah waved his wrist, at a loss for words. "Athletic?"

"Um…" Adam pursed his lips. "I'm not sure what you're getting at, buddy."

Yeah, where was anyone supposed to take that? He needed to be clear. "Do you think he smokes?"

"Oh. Cigarettes?" Adam's forehead bunched. "I have no clue."

Noah rubbed his chin, unsure why he was asking Adam instead of talking to Teagan—except for that whole stepping-across-the-line problem. Talking to Adam like this probably wasn't going to help. "Never mind. I was just making generalizations. They won't help me, anyway."

Adam looked no less confused than when Noah had first turned the conversation to the topic of Teagan. "Won't help you with Teagan? Are you two…?"

"Yes. No. Not like that. We have an agreement that…" Noah had no idea how to explain what he could barely understand himself at that moment. How they had agreed to mutual disinterest, for the sake of the kids. "We have an agreement."

"I see."

Noah was glad Adam did, because Noah was getting more confused by the minute. "If her ex-husband was bothering her, I'd have a problem. That's all."

"Huh." Adam wandered the small room then turned back to Noah. "I wish I had something to add, but I can't say I've heard a word that'd be helpful. The guy is in and out of town—with BS tales of adventure—and only here long enough to wash clothes, restock accessories, and keep his licenses up to date."

All were good reasons for a water-dwelling guy to keep an old home base handy. "Makes sense."

"I wish I could help. Anything else?" Adam asked. "Or I can show you our new trail maps if you want to take anyone you're *not* interested in out for a hike."

Color hit Noah's cheeks. It was one thing to talk about Teagan in a protective manner. It was another to discuss date planning, especially since he didn't know how much to hang with her. "How about Nuts and Bolts? I'm open for business, and nobody knows."

"Oh, come on." Adam's forehead furrowed. "You've been

back for less than a month. It took a long time to pull together the youth camp."

"I have to pay bills and figure out how to generate income from a business that's been shuttered."

"People will hear that Nuts and Bolts is open. By the time Halloween comes around, they'll see it in the parade."

Halloween felt a lifetime away. Noah rubbed his temple. "You're right."

Adam paced quietly around the backroom. "How about I help spread the word?"

"That'd be huge."

"Great. If they can drive it, I'll tell them to head your way."

Noah's shoulders relaxed, and he hadn't realized how tense they'd been. The burden of carrying for someone other than himself was weighing heavy on him. Not that he didn't think he could do it, but he wanted to do more than just rely on what his family could provide. He wanted to be successful in his own right. "Let them know I can fix anything. ATVs, four wheelers." He dropped his gaze pointedly. "Surfski trailers, I can service those too."

"Consider it done."

"Sweet." This was a business deal. Maybe not a big one, but it'd been a small step of marketing his place. It was what he'd read about and needed to do more of, and the thought made cool prickles of sweat dampen the back of his polo shirt's collar. It was a small victory, but he'd take it. Should he do more? Hell, Noah had no idea what to do. His heart rate picked up from nerves—adrenaline, maybe, but not from discomfort. Never in a hundred missions that would scare the hair off a man's chest had he thought twice about what he'd just considered a win, and now he was filled with doubt.

"If you want, I could tack on an A To Z discount," Noah offered. "Just have them mention you sent them my way."

Man, he hated sales. It was the dirty word he hadn't known existed. But if nothing else, the military had trained him to persevere.

"Seriously." Adam gave a confused double take. "You don't have to offer a discount. Consider it done."

Noah blinked, recalibrating his next move. He thought of the business expert planning guides he'd pored over. They'd told him to always expect a phase two when discussing business, marketing, and sales, even in casual conversations. *Take the customer's objection and play to their needs.* But Adam hadn't objected, and nothing Noah had researched said an immediate acceptance of his business offer was a remote possibility, even from family and friends. "Okay, then."

"We covered business, life, and love today," Adam cracked as he led them toward the reception area. "Was that it? Or did we miss any other major life moments?"

"I'll pay you back for the help with Nuts and Bolts. Somehow." Noah's loosened shoulders tensed again. "Make it worth your while."

Adam stopped and leaned against the wall that separated the reception area from the main entry. "You've been in DC too long, buddy. Take a day. Hit the trails, ride the rapids, get some fresh air. Do something."

Noah grumbled, never having considered himself a Washington insider. "Meaning?"

"I don't want anything in return. Zane won't, either."

"Thanks, but—"

"It's a good deal to offer our customers someone we trust who's close by, but that's not why we'd do it." His eyes narrowed. "We're going to help you out. Everybody in Eagle's

Ridge will."

Noah let that churn then recalled the fire chief's refusal to take a free service call for his team. They felt bad for him? Why? Because Lainey had died? Or because he'd left his SEAL team? It couldn't have been because he had Bella now, because how could that be a bad thing. "I don't want pity work, either."

Adam scoffed. "*I* know that wasn't directed at me."

Noah shoved his shoulders up, tossing his hands in the air, clueless.

"Maybe you forgot where you came from."

"Like hell."

"But there's a reason this town was rooted in service and integrity. There's a reason people come home. You came home."

"I couldn't tell Lainey and Bella no."

"No kidding, Noah. Your integrity—and not pity—will be the reason customers stop by when they find out you're open. I know you'll do an excellent job, and they want to support local businesses."

"You're like a freaking commercial," he grumbled to keep from choking up.

But he was right. Eagle's Ridge was more than HALO pancakes and Founders' Day memories. Their childhood had been peppered with facts about the town, like how Sentinel Bridge had four soldiers guard it, connecting the good and bad sides of town under the protective eye of warriors, or how No Man's Land was more than just the perfect meeting space for families and friends because it was considered neutral ground.

Every tale had a backstory that made it larger than life but always left a lesson. At least that was what his mother had told him—to ignore the gossip, focus on the takeaways, and remember that their town was founded on loyalty, the values that their great-grandfathers had instilled when they climbed to the top of a rock to scout out land parcels and spotted a Bald Eagle.

Noah let the community's history and Adam's words settle over him. "I hadn't thought about it like that."

The front door opened as Gambler nosed in, followed by Zane. "Hey, Noah."

He dropped to his knees to give Gambler a scrub on his head. "What's up, guys?"

"How goes parental duty?" Zane watched Gambler lick Noah then come back to his side.

"Not too bad." He shoved his hands into his pockets, nodding toward Zane's twin. "Adam just put life into perspective, so ... room for improvement."

Zane slapped him on the back. "Showing off the surfski?"

They cracked up, exciting Gambler, who jumped up and ran around Zane before he plopped down again.

"Don't underestimate that thing," Zane continued. "But it's a rush."

"Looks it." Noah grinned. "Like I said to Adam, I'm a boss. So..." He shrugged. "It'll be a snap."

"Sure." Gambler stood up and nuzzled his head into Zane's hand. "While you're so busy crushing it, why don't you tell me where you're living. I heard you burned Lainey's house down to the foundation."

"Hildie tell you that?" Noah shook his head.

"Not much changes." Zane ruffled Gambler's head. "Except this guy didn't like Hildie's sweater, so I couldn't stick around for the part where you had to be rescued. Carried out, was it?"

They laughed at the exaggeration, and Noah finally added,

"It keeps getting legs. Next thing you know, someone's going to ask me if Eagle's Ridge still exists."

Adam snorted. "All because you tried to cook Bailey's casserole."

CHAPTER SIXTEEN

TEAGAN GLANCED UP from the papers strewn across her desk. The office secretary, Alexis, hovered by the doorjamb as though she had far more in mind than teacher-lounge gossip or carpool chitchat. With a small checkmark on her to-do list and a sticky note where she was leaving off in her pile of work, Teagan eased back in her chair.

"So…" Alexis slinked around the open door and leaned back, her arms crossed to make her long, brilliantly colored sweater cocoon around her.

"Hey, what's going on?" Teagan twirled a pen between her fingers.

Alexis fanned herself. "*So…*"

The pen froze mid-bobble. "*Yes?*"

"There is a very thick, very rugged man sitting in the waiting room and making a few teachers thirsty."

Teagan blushed but offered nothing more than an "Oh" at what had to be Noah's unexpected visit.

"He's asked to see you."

This was going to make Hildie's afternoon gossip report if Teagan didn't stop blushing. "Did he mention who his child—"

"He said nothing about a student and referenced a personal matter." Alexis wriggled her eyebrows. "You're not even asking who he is. I'm going to need the details."

Well played, Alexis. "We'll talk later, and I'll be out in a minute." Teagan reached for her purse in the bottom drawer. It didn't take long to throw on a fresh application of pale lipstick, run a brush through her hair, and tuck the bag away before she stood to nervously smooth her shirt and her skirt over her hips.

Freshening her face was silly. The butterflies somersaulting in her stomach were equally as ridiculous. Still, with every step forward, her anticipation grew. By the time she was ready to head around the corner to the waiting area, the easy walk made her feel breathless.

Noah sat on a bench in the main office, where Teagan had met thousands of parents before. *A thousand fathers before.* This was the first time her steps slowed when the man looked up.

Noah stood, and his greeting was warm yet reserved. His tense shoulders remained stiff as his jawline. "Sorry to drop in on you. I called, but you didn't answer."

Teagan flipped her hand nervously. "Sorry, I only check my phone on breaks and lunch. Is everything okay?" Alexis would have notified her if a parent had requested an emergency meeting.

"Can we...?" He glanced about the open area where any-one could walk through.

"Sure. Come back to my office, and we'll chat." She re-traced her steps with Noah following, and the excited bundle of nerves she felt on the way out had been replaced with unease. Had she been wrong to reach out to him, hoping that it was Noah in her backyard?

She could see why that might feel like a needy attempt for attention. Embarrassed warmth hit her cheeks at the thought that he might suspect a professional woman in her thirties of playing silly games. "This is my office."

He followed her in and took a seat as she rounded the

desk. A grim cast came over his handsome features, and she knew this conversation would be uncomfortable. He had come from work to make sure she understood where their boundaries were. It was definitely one of her more humiliating moments.

"About the call last night," she started. "I'm sorry. I shouldn't have—"

"Yes, you should." Noah inched forward in his chair. "I want that to be clear before we say anything else."

Teagan swallowed over the knot in her throat. "Of course."

He repositioned and straightened, as though he didn't want to be there any more than she wanted to hear him call her out for an overactive imagination. "About last night…"

She couldn't handle the thought that he might believe she'd placed that call because she couldn't stay away from him or needed his attention. Embarrassed, she clasped her hands under her desk. "I know you think that I called you as though you were my knight in shining armor, but those noises were real, and I was worried—"

"Stop."

She blinked rapidly, choking on her words.

"Teagan, I know." Noah pulled his chair closer to the desk. "But after what I'm going to tell you, I don't know if you'll ever call me again."

HERE WENT NOTHING. Noah pictured the best way to explain how he'd overstepped the bounds of a normal *friendship* last night. Nothing came to mind as his gaze drifted over her shoulder to a pennant from the homecoming football game.

That was an example he could work with. Maybe. "Have you ever taken the ball and…" Noah gripped an imaginary football, staring at his empty hands, then tucked it to his chest.

Teagan obviously had not. He put one arm out, as if he was blocking and shielding, twisting and flexing the arm-carrying ball for emphasis. "And run with it?"

"Is that a football?" She gestured to the empty space under his armpit.

"Aren't counselors trained to use their imagination?" He dropped his arm and let the football disappear from his thoughts.

With a gentle tilt of her head, Teagan cast a sideways glance through her eyelashes. "I'm ninety-five percent sure that you didn't come here to discuss football."

He snickered despite what he had to tell her. "You're giving me a five percent chance of cutting work and interrupting your day to talk about sports?"

"I think so, yes."

He leaned back. "Do I come off as a sports guy?"

A flirtatious eyebrow lift teased him. "Noah, you come off as a do-whatever-you-want kind of guy."

"Well…" He angled his head, losing his focus on why he was there.

"If sports were on your mind, and you wanted to discuss them." She nodded. "Yes, I think we'd have that discussion."

Wouldn't be the first time his dominant nature had gotten him in a situation. "But not in a barbaric, caveman, ruin-your-job and interrupt-your-day kind of way," he said. He wasn't a Neanderthal, though he had shown up to discuss overstepping what some might call boundaries and was dropping football references. "Maybe you're on to something."

"I don't doubt your best intentions," she said. "But why won't I call you again?"

Well, hell. Again, here went nothing. "When you called

me last night, I wasn't comfortable with how you sounded."

Teagan's sweet smile quickly sobered. "I called because I wasn't comfortable."

"I called my buddy, Wyatt. He knows people around town and connected with local PD."

Teagan's eyes went wide. "You did what?"

Despite the shock on her face, Noah kept plowing. "I asked Wyatt to swing over to my place."

"Last night?" Teagan blinked rapidly, stammering. "Why?"

"Wyatt knows Bella, and if Bella woke up, he could easily explain that I had to run out."

"Run out?" Her eyes stopped the rapid-fire blinks and froze. "Where did you run out to?"

Noah stifled an uncertain groan, staring at a crack in the ceiling. He might have overreacted, but he would do it over and over again, faced with the same situation. He faced her head-on. "Your place."

"*Mine?*"

"I wanted to check it out." Noah squared his shoulders and would stand by every action he'd taken. "I know that sounds crazy. Overprotective. Overbearing. Even saying it aloud, it's… a lot. But at the time, the way your voice shook, Teagan, you sounded scared."

Her lips parted before she closed them again. Not the best reaction, though it was better than her standing and screaming "stalker."

"Thank you," she whispered quietly. "I wanted to ask you to come over. But… Bella." Her eyes went to her desk. "There was no one else I trusted enough, but I just turned the lights out."

"I should've told you I was coming." She would've felt better.

With a quick flick of her wrist, Teagan downplayed the situation for his benefit. "Nothing came of it, so…"

"Damn it, I should've told you."

"Noah, really. That means a lot to me."

He ran a hand over his chin. He didn't have the best of news to follow up with. "I didn't see anyone back there, but there was another issue."

Teagan crossed her arms, and worry marred her forehead. "What kind of issue?"

"I saw a pile of cigarette butts that struck me as out of place."

"Really?"

"I mentioned it to Wyatt, he mentioned it to his friend at the police department, and they dropped by your place today while you were at school."

Her eyes widened. "And?"

"I think we were all hoping your lawn guy ditched his cigarette butts in the same corner every week or something." Noah shook his head. "The detective took a close look at them in the daylight, and they look smoked about the same time frame."

Teagan's mouth gaped. "Someone sat outside my house, smoking?"

He nodded. "And your shed."

"What about it?"

"On the inside, the insulation had been torn out. Does that make any sense?"

Her face skewed. "Like an animal got into the wall?"

That'd been his hope too. "Not so much. More like it was stripped out."

Teagan bit her lip. "I never use that old shed. There's nothing in there. My ex-husband built it to store some equipment and gadgets. That's why it was insulated, but I haven't used it in years." Her brow furrowed.

Interesting. "Last night, before I got home, I ran into your neighborhood watch."

"We don't have a neighborhood watch." Her bottom lip trembled.

"Know anyone named Edward Lee?"

Teagan shook her head. "No."

That was what Lexi and her husband Parker, an elite hacker Lexi's equal, had turned up too. That person didn't exist in Eagle's Ridge, much less Teagan's neighborhood.

"But…"

Noah's eyebrows arched as panic set in on her face. "What, Teagan?"

"But Edward Lee was often my ex-husband's screen name."

His brow furrowed. "What? Why?"

"It's some guy. E. Lee. First name's Edward, but his last name's Spence. He's an underwater archaeologist."

"A what?" he asked.

"Another treasurer hunter."

Had Noah run into Teagan's husband? Talked to the bastard? But why? What was going on?

"Was he at my house?" she asked.

Noah's mind couldn't keep up, but he would loop the detective in. "Does he smoke?"

Teagan shook her head. "No. He never did."

"I don't know what's going on, but awareness is half the battle. If there's an issue, Eagle's Ridge PD has been clued in and will be on the lookout now."

Teagan looked numb—or maybe shocked.

"Your street will be on their patrol."

"For what?" she asked.

"Exactly. There hasn't been a crime committed. Other than the damage to the inside of the shed."

"And who knows when that damage happened? I haven't opened that thing in a long time."

They sat in silence, and Noah let Teagan work through everything he had told her, waiting for her to set aside what he had shared and flip out over what he had done. But that didn't happen.

"Why are you looking at me like that?" she finally asked.

Ha. He could start a list. The easiest answer was that she was gorgeous. Her expressive eyes made him react in half a dozen ways. She could curl her lips, and Noah would be lust-drunk or laughing. Looking at her was a top favorite pastime, but that wasn't what she meant. "I was worried."

"About last night?"

"Nah, stuff like that doesn't faze me."

"Then what?"

"I didn't know how you'd react to me. Reacting to you." He inched forward, resting his forearms on her desk, and simply watched as her chest rose and fell more than it had when he first arrived. Their dynamic squeezed him from the inside out, and now he could see that it did her too.

What he wouldn't give to run his hands over her, to feel that she was safe. *That* was why he was staring, because he was longing.

"And what's that look for?" Teagan asked in a much quieter, coarser voice.

His hungry gaze dropped, and Noah inhaled deeply before braving a look at her again. "After all the sharing just now, I'm going to keep that to myself."

He stood before he could say or do anything that would

cross a clearly set line. Last night's line was a guess. The one in his mind was specific, and she didn't want to cross it again.

They had kissed, and she'd said pull back.

Teagan was comfortable with their relationship as friends, and that was where he would leave it. "I'll catch you later. Call me if you need anything."

Then Noah forced himself from her office with the knowledge that one day, they would be a couple. He just needed to back up and let what he knew to be fact catch up with reality.

CHAPTER SEVENTEEN

THE LEGO TOWER now rivaled Will in height and spanned the length of his arms as Teagan sat on the couch in an old pair of sweatpants and an Eagle's Ridge track T-shirt. She watched one tower sway as her son quickly leaped into action to fortify the base. Only when she was sure that his hours of work wouldn't crash did she go back to her review of IEPs.

Schoolteachers were finishing interims, and she was keeping an eye on the progress of the new school year start of individual plans for students who needed special help with programs. There was never enough time and resources.

Knock, knock.

Will jumped. "Someone's at the door! Oh no!"

The tower of blocks, which he had just stabilized, toppled and crashed. Legos shot in every direction, and his cheeks flushed to a frustrated red. "They broke, Mama. I—"

"Don't say anything you might regret, otherwise all the Legos go up."

He swallowed what looked to be one hundred kindergarten versions of "shoot" and plopped to the ground to start rebuilding.

"Good decision." She set her work on the coffee table and headed toward the door, hoping whoever it was had a fantastic reason that she could give Will for the knocking. "Coming."

Padding down the hallway barefoot, she rolled her pants

once to keep them on her hips then opened the door. The world froze.

"Teagan, it's great to see you," her ex-husband said on the front porch of the home they used to share before he so cavalierly walked out when she had a newborn in her arms.

How they had managed to avoid each other for five years, she had no idea. Even though Spencer traveled almost constantly, he still called Eagle's Ridge home. But this was not his house. "What are you doing here?"

"I was hoping to come in and chat."

She inched out of the door, squeezing it almost shut behind her. "Are you out of your mind? You can't come here."

"I didn't think we parted on those kinds of terms."

"Were you in my neighborhood recently?" she snapped.

Spencer shook his head. "I was in town a couple weeks ago but not over here. Why?"

"A friend thought he saw you."

Spencer took a step closer. "Did he? How would he know it was me?"

"Because of *Edward Lee*. Was that you?"

He pushed a hand against the door. "Let me in, Tea."

She balked, bumping into the door and clattering for the handle to pull it back again. Will didn't need to see him. He'd never met his father, and right now wasn't going to be the time that introduction took place, if ever. "No," she hissed. "You walked away. Not even a fight for custody."

The only thing he'd requested was that Teagan notify him before she sold her house, which she'd owned before he moved in with her. If "moving in with" was even a correct description of their living arrangements, considering how often he'd been gone. The judge had given him the right to one final walk-through if she ever sold, for nostalgic purposes.

Her attorney told her to keep quiet, that it was one of the best divorce agreements he'd ever seen. That did nothing but piss her off, though.

Spencer stepped back. "You're making a scene."

"You need to leave."

Will called for her from the living room, and Teagan's blood formed icicles. "Go. Now."

"That's Will, huh? Sounds like a real big kid now."

"Spencer Shaw, get off my property, so help me God."

Spence's cocky smile hung on his tan face, and his sun-bleached hair hung over his eyes in a way that said he'd spent too much time on the beach lately. Yet still he managed to wear nice clothing and, from the looks of the car parked in front of the house, had a nice ride. There were so many questions surrounding him that she'd never wanted to think about again.

"Hey, let me hit the bathroom real quick. Just tell him I'm a salesperson. Doesn't matter."

Doesn't matter. Her heart shattered. It didn't matter. To Spence, it didn't. But to Will, it would. His heart would splinter, knowing that his long-lost father wanted to use the bathroom more than he wanted to meet his son.

Her eyelids burned with tears, and Teagan couldn't manage the words "Go to hell." She simply stumbled back and slammed the door shut.

CHAPTER EIGHTEEN

B USINESS WAS FINALLY picking up at Nuts and Bolts, and Noah had a sense of accomplishment. Not only was he using his hands as he had in demolition, tinkering and troubleshooting to finally tune parts that should flow together effortlessly, but he'd found satisfaction as a new business owner. Entrepreneurship wasn't Noah's calling, though. Providing for others was. It would've been a bold-faced lie to say he had the slightest interest in accounting or marketing. Putting in hours long after Bella was asleep to learn what came beyond the basics of Business 101 made for tediously long nights, but he was in it for the long haul.

He poured lotion on his hands and wiped the grease off on a cloth then tossed it over his shoulder. He'd earned enough this week to not be in the hole. There was a trust and savings to rely on, but his personal goals made him work hard so he wouldn't rely on those as if he were starting from scratch. Maybe it was too hard and idealistic for some, but dammit, he was going to do it.

This was his life now. No more jumps out of a helicopter, no surfacing in the water on a strike. He wouldn't search for enemies, couldn't calculate for explosions and demolitions. It was a time of transition, and Noah found himself making lists of normal, everyday activities.

He planned to meet Wyatt at Baldie's for beers later in the

week. He wanted to invite the guys over to the house after he made it more of his own place. Noah had signed up to read a story to Bella's class and was responsible for donating the classroom pumpkin. He downloaded the phone app for the school's sports booster program even though Bella was too young to participate in any of the Eagle's Ridge school athletic activities. At least he could track the high school scores, which was a topic of local conversation. All day long, Noah talked to customers and business associates, but at the end of the day, before Bella walked off the bus, an unfamiliar loneliness continued to surround him at his house.

He had connections, but they weren't personal. Other than Bella. And Teagan—even Will. But he wanted more depth with Teagan. More warmth. More of her. More everything.

Noah dropped to his desk chair and stared blankly at a pile of work.

He took his phone out of his desk drawer and didn't know who to reach out to, particularly when he had nothing to say. That used to be Lainey, who was there for the few and far between times when he needed somebody to just get him. He scrolled the contact list and swiped Teagan's name. She didn't fit the bill as a makeshift replacement for Lainey, but he didn't want to replace his cousin and didn't feel as if Teagan needed to adapt to fit a role, or that he needed a reason to talk to her.

Much like Lainey.

She answered on the second ring, but the tone of her hello changed his self-focused reflection to an immediate concern that something was wrong. "Teagan, what's the matter?"

She grumbled. "That easy to tell? Great. Just peachy."

"Rotten day at work?" How bad could it be in an elementary school? It wasn't as if she could be called to the principal's office.

"It's just a weird two days. I haven't heard from my ex-husband in years, and yesterday he shows up and wants to chat. Today the same thing."

Noah's lips flattened, and he wasn't sure how best to answer as a platonic friend. "What's he want?"

"I can tell you what he doesn't want. To see Will. Which is fine by me, but it's also heartbreaking."

Noah shook his head. "Is there anything I can do?"

"Is it weird that I'm talking to you about him?"

"Why would that be weird?"

"People have preconceived notions about Spence, and frankly, I don't want to talk to them about him."

He ignored the solid river of irritation punching in his jugular. "I'll listen to anything."

"Thanks. I—Hang on a second." The phone muffled as he waited. "Someone popped into my office, and I have to jump. But this afternoon I'm headed over to the middle school for a counselors' meeting, then I'm done for the day. Maybe I could swing by Nuts and Bolts? I'll bring coffee."

She could show up throwing spitballs and dropping stink bombs, and Noah wouldn't send her packing. "You don't have to bring coffee. But I won't say no."

"Sweet! I'll see you later."

They said their goodbyes, and he hung up. He tossed the phone onto his desk amid the spreadsheets and orders that he needed to catalog. He hadn't ever been this excited to sit at his desk and do nothing. Considering their topic of conversation, though, it would take effort to behave like a gentleman. Hell, who'd said anything in their agreement about gentlemanly behavior? Maybe he could be the type of friend who could bounce an ex-husband out of town on his ass.

Didn't every woman need that kind of man in her life?

Yeah, Noah was pretty sure they did, and that was who he was going to be. The ass-kicking acquaintance of the beautiful Teagan Shaw.

CHAPTER NINETEEN

THE PITTER-PATTER OF Teagan's heart drummed louder than the bass on the radio. Her stomach was in knots, and her pulse jumped erratically at the recall of Noah's baritone voice pressed against her ear.

Her excitement level was at an all-time high, buzzing from the second she hung up with him and growing to the point that when she stopped for their coffees, she ordered hers as decaf.

Nuts and Bolts loomed closer, and the simple act of signaling to turn made her smile. "Stop it."

Especially given the topic. It wasn't as if Teagan could bounce into Noah's office, glowing as she was now, and expect to discuss Spencer. Noah would think... Who knew what he would think? She didn't know what to think.

Spencer had terrified her and broken her heart all over again by how he acted toward Will. Not that she wanted him near her son. But she was giddy to see Noah.

She turned in to the parking lot and let the Subaru idle before shifting into Park and shutting off the engine. "He's your friend."

Teagan checked the rearview mirror for the hundredth time then grabbed her purse and the two coffees before sliding out the car door.

Noah was at the front door, an arm overhead and propped

against the doorjamb as he leaned his long frame against the wall. Teagan's confident first step slowed. She didn't expect him there. Didn't expect anyone who looked like that, with long arms and thick muscles, to stare at her. Then he smiled, and her heart tried to also, expanding in her chest before her lips got with the program.

"Hey, need a hand?" He pushed off the wall, letting the door swing closed.

"Sure."

He took the coffee from her and rested a hand on the small of her back, guiding her toward the door, then he held it open as a cold wind blustered.

Inside the warm office, Teagan finger combed her hair back and he set the coffees down, offering to take her jacket. They took their drinks to his office.

Noah's office was just like the rest of the shop, kind of quirky. A sign behind his desk read:

Ratta-Tat-Tat $10

Ka-Plunk Ka-Plunk $20

Ping-Ping Thud-Thud $30

And the wrench clock and license plate light shades didn't look his style, but he was smart enough to keep the place the way that it had been. Eagle's Ridge loved it.

"I've heard business has been doing well," she said.

"It's picking up." He leaned back in his chair. "Are you going to tell me, or do I begin my list of what-happened-with-Spencer questions?"

Teagan groaned. "I hate that man. Or maybe not. You have to love to hate."

Noah took a sip of his coffee.

"He showed up and wanted to come on in and chat. The nerve of him. Didn't even say hi to Will. Not like that's how I'd want to introduce him to his father, but he wasn't interested."

"He was interested in you?" Noah bobbed his brows.

Teagan thought back on it. "No. I don't know what his deal was. He just wanted to come in."

"Did he?"

"No."

"Do you feel safe?" Noah asked.

"From Spencer? Sure. He just makes me so... angry."

"Because of Will."

Her eyes burned, and she focused on her coffee. "Because it's not fair that I was so stupid. He's such an amazing kid." Tears slipped free. I *want* him to have a dad. It wasn't like I thought that Spencer would be gone. Never like this." Teagan wiped her cheeks then realized who she was talking to. "God, I must sound so selfish. Here you are when Bella's lost both her parents. You've given up your career."

Noah stood from his chair, walked to her side of the desk, and sat on the edge. He took her coffee cup from her and wrapped his arms around her back, hugging her to his chest. "Don't do that."

She couldn't help it. Teagan never let her guard down or knew she needed to. But with Noah she could. "I just wish my baby had a life without the threat of heartache. Isn't that what every mom wants for her children?" She sniffed. "And his father was so close. He was there. He *heard* Will and just didn't care."

The tears fell, and Noah hugged her until she stopped. Her thoughts cleared. His unhesitating hand rubbed her back slowly until she dabbed at her eyes again.

"Sorry about that." Teagan straightened in her seat as he handed over her coffee. "I didn't think I was coming here to fall apart."

"You're fine."

She chuckled. "That's my job. Listening while others unbottle their problems. I think you have better things to do."

"Than make sure you feel better?" His forehead bunched. "Shit, no." The front door of Nuts and Bolts jingled. "Hang on a second. I wasn't expecting anyone right now."

Noah stepped into the reception area, and Teagan peeked out as he greeted Augie Kensington. They spoke for a moment then disappeared after Noah grabbed a set of keys off the wall and went outside.

Teagan used the time alone to open her purse and take out a compact, check her smeared eye makeup, and fix it as best she could. She heard the men come back and a transaction finalize before Noah came back in.

"Before you know it, this place will be slammed." She put her compact back in her purse and dropped it on the floor.

"That guy has a nice ride," Noah said. "So far I've tuned up pickup trucks and minivans."

"Well, pencil in a Subaru in the next couple weeks."

"As long as Will can come by and help. I promised him he could work on your car."

Every ounce of her wanted to hug him. Forget the sexy man and all his muscles that leaned against the door like the Diet Coke man from the long-ago commercial. Noah was so much more than she could ever have hoped for… in a friend. She just wanted to hold onto him and never let go. "Thank you, Noah. I'm not sure of everything I'm thanking you for. I just know it's a lot."

CHAPTER TWENTY

THERE WAS A distinct difference between Halloweens of years past and this one. Suddenly Noah had a whole new appreciation for costumes, and it wasn't for the better as Bella dragged him through the front doors of the general store. The realization that Halloween had become a grown-up, hyped-up holiday of oversexualization and nothing to do with kids' fun was a boot in the chest. He waved to the cashier he went to grade school with and followed Bella down the first aisle.

He took a deep breath when witches and warlocks greeted them. There were no sexy vampires or pirates who wanted to show off their booties. Instead, there was row after row of colorful princesses, muscled and padded heroes, and storybook villains. A quick swell of relief rolled through him as some of the more recognizable characters caught his eye. This might even be easy.

Bella skipped and stopped, stared at her options, then started her process again as Noah donned a mask then mimicked her inspection.

"Hey, ladybug." He readjusted his face mask to see out of the two small eyeholes. "Are you thinking a fairy princess or superhero?"

With shiny-stringed wands in each hand, she spun on her toe. "Not sure."

When in Rome… He picked up his own magical princess

wands with the shiny strings—which he had to admit had an instant fun factor—and waved them side to side like handheld flags. "I think this is my costume. Scary mask, cute hands. What do you think?"

"It suits you."

It suits you. What five-year-old spoke like that? But she was right. It did suit him, so who was he to question. There were far too many options that looked eerily the same. If he didn't want to be here all night, Noah needed a plan. He decided that narrowing his options for her would be the best course of action. "Were you thinking a color scheme? Or characters?"

Bella's wand-swirling arms fell as if they'd been tied to anchors in the river.

"What?" he asked.

"You want me to choose by color?" Her sweet face skewed.

"Kidding. Kinda." Who knew he would be happy to be hiding behind a ghoul's mask from a five-year-old's displeasure. "Then character it is. Are we filtering by powers or favorite movie—"

"Where is the people section?"

He'd never been one to miss the obvious, but staring back at him appeared to be people—princesses, princes, knights, and police officers. There was Army. Notably missing were the Navy SEALs. Two different fireman costumes hung side by side, and there were several costumes for service industry characters, including chefs, bakers, and railroad engineers. All in all, Noah saw people. "I think we're here, kid."

Her wand-holding hands went to her hips. She was still not pleased. "No, real people."

"Ladybug, these are all real people. And when you wear their costume, you will make them come alive." Wasn't that the point of Halloween? Some kids wanted to go "Boo."

Others wanted to emulate their heroes. There was a missing piece of the Halloween puzzle, though, and for the life of him, Noah couldn't see what seemed so obvious to her. "Is there a specific person you're looking for? From a movie? Or a job?"

"The girl in the picture with all the books who put the man on the moon."

"Buzz Aldrin? That was a man and—"

"No." Her little face scowled. "The girl who wrote the program that put him there. She did it with a pencil. And there were lots of books. That's who I want to be for Halloween."

There was Halloween shopping for kids, and then there was Halloween shopping for Bella. Noah understood this to be true and now realized he needed help. More importantly, he might also need a history lesson because he had obviously missed a chapter while learning how the first man had walked on the moon. "Give me a second."

Noah stuck both of his shiny wands in his back pocket, exchanged one of them for his cell phone, and opened up the search browser. Keywords for his image search were "girl books man on the moon."

The results were woefully disappointing with pictures of musical acts that this little ladybug better not know about.

Noah tried again with "code NASA female staff." That time the images were far more appropriate, yet there was nothing that would seem to satisfy Bella's upturned, imploring eyes.

"Did you find it?" She was surrounded by nothing that interested her, but the hope in her voice was enough to slice through his gut.

"Getting closer. I'll figure it out." His gaze lifted behind her as the simple encouragement caused her to beam far more than the shiny wands had. "And if they don't have it here, I'll see where they do have it."

Her eyes cast down as her shoulders drooped. "What if they don't have it anywhere?"

Another gut shot, delivered in stealth mode by his little ladybug. "I know you didn't ask if there was something I couldn't do." He clucked lightly and dropped to his knees. Chuckling quietly, he said, "If I have to hand stitch the thing, you will be it."

Whoever "it" was. That was first and foremost in this operation—figure out his target.

Noah hated to think that Teagan might assume he was using her only for help, but this situation was about to be at Mayday level.

"Go play for a few minutes while I do a little more research." And by research, he meant texting his resource on all things… Well, all things at this point in time.

NOAH: *Mayday, Mayday. I need Halloween help.*

His phone flashed with an immediate notification and text message back. Noah wasn't sure whether he was more thrilled for the help or to see her name flash onto his screen.

TEAGAN: *I'm doing Halloween right now too. What's up?*

NOAH: *Costumes. Or a specific costume.*

TEAGAN: *LOL*

NOAH: *This is the description I'm working with. A girl who handwrote the book that put somebody on the moon.*

He hit Send and reread his text. It was so generic but at the same time so specific, what was he missing? And he didn't want Teagan to think he was taking the lazy way out and simply texting her, or texting her just because. Now he felt like a schoolkid with a crush.

NOAH: *I promise. I Googled.*

TEAGAN: *Here you go.*

The image accompanying her text message was exactly as Bella had described. A young woman stood with a stack of books that was nearly as tall as she was. The caption on the picture read "Margaret Hamilton handwrote the code for NASA's Apollo mission."

He had a huge grin on his face. There were so many reasons. That was who Bella wanted to be for Halloween? Hell yes. She made him so proud, and Lainey would be proud too. Thank God for the ghoul's mask, because his eyes stung for a moment as he thought about how excited she would've been to create that costume for her daughter. But Noah also smiled because Teagan knew. She knew Bella, she knew amazing things, and she was able to share with him without making him feel like a jackass.

He closed the image and saw another text message from her.

TEAGAN: *Doubtful you will find *this* costume but I can help pull one together if you like.*

"Will!" Bella trotted down the aisle as Noah glanced up to see Teagan round the corner with an armful of supplies.

"How funny," Teagan said, laughing.

Will and Bella greeted each other with raucous surprise then put their heads together, breaking apart a second later.

"Excuse us," Bella said. "We have a potion to make."

"A potion, huh?" Noah swept his arm out, granting them permission to pass toward the witches section of the store.

Will scowled at Noah's antics. "It's very serious. You

shouldn't laugh."

"Life-fault-ernating." Bella was as unimpressed with Noah as Will.

"Tough crowd," Noah mumbled to himself, then he beckoned Bella closer. "Alternating? Meaning, changing?"

"Yes," Will gravely answered for Bella then tilted his head toward Teagan. "Are you alternating your life?"

"I could alternate, little man." Her amusement was barely hidden by her serious tone.

"*Phew.*" Will let out a heavy sigh of relief.

"Phew!" Bella repeated as she jumped, then they raced to the head of the aisle as Teagan called for them to walk.

"They're almost as relieved as I was to learn you know who Margaret Hamilton was," he said.

Teagan stepped to his side, and they watched Bella and Will speed walk to the closest witches' brooms and find their place among the cauldrons in the store aisle, pretending to pour imaginary bottles as they stirred their potions.

Will jumped back from what seemed to be an imaginary pot boiling over, and together they lifted an apparently heavy container and dumped it into the pot.

"Active imaginations." Noah glanced down at Teagan by his side then flipped the phone in his hand. He pocketed it as Teagan covered her laughter with her hand, but she wasn't watching the kids. "What?"

"You," she said. "In the mask."

"Me?" He flipped out his hands but egged on her laughter as he tilted his covered face, as though he were unaware of what he looked like. "What?"

"Even if I didn't expect to see you here, I could've guessed who was behind the ghoul's mask."

"Rwar," he joked.

"But I certainly didn't expect to see you with sequin-and-string fairy godmother wands trailing from your backside."

Ha! He'd forgotten! "These bad boys?"

Noah did a quick strut-and-spin, positive he made the sequin and strings shake as he turned around.

Her eyes danced. "It's a good look for you. Softens the fangs and hairiness."

"You like the ghoul's mask."

"I like your face better," she said quietly.

Something about her tone quickly ran through him, how the humor was gone and how she seemed to be standing closer. He slid the mask off, running his hands into his hair that he was letting grow longer.

"Much more handsome."

Simple and innocent, but it hit him straight in the chest. She made his blood warm and his need for her jump.

They had agreed their kiss was born out of stress and worry, curiosity and misplaced tension. Noah only wanted to do what was right for Bella. Family came first. But taking care of Bella didn't mean that he could ignore needs and desires. That Noah was alive and that every inch of him was aware of Teagan. Not just how her cheeks were still pink after she said he was handsome or the way her hair fell around her face but the sound of her voice and the sweetness of her intentions. Hell, her looks were simply a bonus, and they didn't explain why her text messages were the best part of his day. Teagan's intelligence and humor, how she cared for her son, for Bella, and her students... for him. Those were the things driving him to the edge.

But they'd already gone down that road, and it was now labeled Restricted. He liked being her friend, and that was what he'd focus on.

"Let me give you a hand with that." Noah lifted the table-cloths and packages of matching cups and plates from her arms. "Changing the motif at home?"

She remained close as she let go of the burden in her arms. "As much easier as plastic plates and cups might be, it's for a school party."

He glanced over his shoulder. Will and Bella were perfectly content to stir their witches' cauldrons without adult interference. "I have some Googling ahead of me to plan the costume. I'm not sure how much of it I'm going to find here." Perfectly safe conversation for friends. He could do this because he had to. Screwing up wasn't an option. Noah chewed the inside of his cheek. "Were you two still shopping or wrapping up?"

An indecipherable emotion appeared on Teagan's face. Her sweet smile remained, but the openness in her eyes became guarded. She shifted her stance, glancing at the kids and taking a step away, reminding Noah how much he hated the distance between them.

Wait...

Did he just miss a cue from Teagan, or was he searching for something that wasn't there? Her voice made his skin prickle with excitement, and she stood close, talking quietly. Then she backed away when he didn't notice.

Because he was a guy. Because he was in over his head. Because there were a million reasons he didn't want to burn this friendship, and because, for Bella's sake—as they'd painfully and honestly realized—he needed Teagan as a resource. Caring for Bella wasn't like an uncle babysitting. He couldn't be a fun time and then disappear. And he didn't want to.

And hell, he was going to mess this up, but the way his chest tightened when she got quiet and smiled... Noah set down the plastic ware and tablecloths. Teagan blushed, her eyes nervously darting about the aisle as though she realized he'd just now caught on, that she'd tried to flirt, and he ruined it. Her eyes dropped to the floor where he placed her belongings, and they stayed there as he took an obvious step forward to resume their closeness.

She didn't move. His heart picked up its pace, drawing heavy beats that surged in his neck. Noah reached for her hand and grinned when her fingers rigidly froze in his palm. He didn't want to twine them together or pull her close. Instead he placed his other hand on top, like a sandwich, then simply held her hand in his.

"Teagan."

"Yes?" She interlaced their fingers slowly then unlaced them, and Noah let his fingers trace the outline of her hand in his palm.

"I lied before, and I don't agree."

Her eyes widened as her hand tensed in his.

He clasped his hands around hers, not playing anymore but simply holding still. "Kissing you was a good thing. I can't get it out of my head. And I want it to happen again."

"I do too," she whispered.

"I get your reservations, and believe me, they make sense. I know you're looking out for Bella and yourself. You should be. And nothing I'm about to say will fall within any rule book or shrink guidelines. But…"

"But what?"

As much as he wanted to touch her, he eased their hands apart. He wanted her to think clearly—he needed her to. He was asking her to break their ground rules, and he couldn't think with his hands on her. "Let's get a babysitter. We can head down to the bar at the Broadleaf for cocktails and then over to Bailey's restaurant. A nice dinner, just the two of us. But—"

He took a breath, ready to lay it all out on the line. What was the point of hiding the truth? If Lainey had taught him anything, more than the SEALs even, it was that life comes at you fast. So fast that he could run into this woman and make plans as fast as they came into his head, not having a clue five minutes before that he might ever make such suggestions. "I've never got a babysitter for a kid before in my life. I don't know how long that takes. I don't have to go into the shop tomorrow. Closed on Sundays. You guys go home, pack a bag. Will can have a slumber party with Bella tonight. Stay with me. I'm not asking you to sleep with me." Noah tucked the loose hair on her cheek behind her ear. "I'll sleep on the couch. I'll sleep on the floor. Out in the car. I've slept in far worse. All I know is that you are a special person, I shouldn't have agreed not to kiss you again. I want you closer than you have been. Spend the night, tonight."

He took a step back and watched for a reaction. She wasn't saying a word. That did not bode well.

"I love the Broadleaf."

Okay, a date. Maybe his slumber party idea was too forward. The woman hadn't wanted to kiss again, and he'd thrown out the suggestion of spending the night together, albeit clearly he meant separate bedrooms. Still… What a moron. But he didn't regret laying it on the line like that and would've done it the same way all over again. "Understood. I read you loud and clear."

Noah was midpivot to check on the kids and save face when Teagan touched his bicep. "Hang on a sec. I wasn't done."

A jagged slice of hope picked up in his chest, making him

wonder whether he hadn't crashed and burned completely.

"I have one condition."

"What's that?" he asked.

Her eyebrows bobbed just enough that he knew something fun was coming. "You have to agree without knowing."

He moved closer. "Can I reserve the right to add a condition under your condition?"

She shook her head. "Nope, it's a condition without contingency, and you have to agree to it without knowing what it is."

Game changer. She was throwing in a whole new level of trust factor now. "Done. I agree."

"*I'm* cooking. You're on cleanup duty. With the exception of whatever the kids clear from the table. As hot of a fantasy as a SEAL and firemen might be, I think I only want to spend the night with you."

CHAPTER TWENTY-ONE

"WE'RE MAKING DESSERT," Teagan announced to Bella and Will, who milled nearby. "Go play, and we'll call you when we're ready."

"When you need help?" Will asked.

"Please," Bella begged.

"Maybe," Noah answered. "Go make yourself gone."

Both ran from the room, and Teagan clucked with her tongue.

"What?"

She gave an approving glance. "I think I just saw *the look*?"

"Do you like that?" He grinned. "I've been working on my I-mean-business stare."

"Impressive." Teagan pulled the reusable grocery bag from the freezer and set it on the counter before extracting two containers of ice cream and one of hand-cranked peanut butter with a label from the small organic grocery store.

Noah watched as she moved through Lainey's kitchen as though it were her own, pulling out the blender and finding a spatula with ease.

"My next look goes something like this." He scrunched his forehead, grimacing, letting his mouth gape, and squeezed his eyes shut.

Teagan paused. "Hmm. What are you trying to convey?"

"How I appreciate that Bella uses words that appear on

college entrance exams, but please wait until I've had my coffee and have my dictionary in hand."

"In that case"—she lifted her spatula, tapping it in the air—"you nailed it."

They laughed, and he perched against the edge of the counter. "Do you need any help?"

She made a face.

"That's your no-thank-you you're-never-living-the-casserole-down face?"

"And I nailed it too." She made the same spatula gesture.

He pretended to glare out the window at the next-door neighbor. "Lainey had told me I could trust whoever that is."

"Oh, you can trust Mrs. Eller."

"Uh-huh."

"But you can also trust her to call 9-1-1 if there is even a question that the authorities might need to be involved." Teagan puttered about the kitchen. "If you think about it, that's not so bad of a quality to have in a neighbor."

Noah fake grumbled. "Don't most nosy neighbors knock on your door with a Bundt cake?"

"She probably had the Bundt cake ready when she saw your house burning down."

Noah grabbed a hand towel and playfully snapped Teagan's wrist. "This is how rumors start."

She stole the towel and tossed it on the counter.

He chuckled. "What are you making, anyway? Chocolate milkshakes?"

Teagan busied herself. "A Lainey favorite."

Noah picked up the carton of ice cream. Except it wasn't. "Hold on. What is this?" Coconut milk *frozen dessert*. Chocolate flavored. He cocked his head, confused. "Coconut milk frozen dessert?" He set the carton down, inspecting the one next to it. Almond milk. Chocolate. "Milk? From almonds?"

"I'm making milkshakes."

"You need *ice cream* to make milkshakes."

She stopped giving another look that he was going to have to master one day and set up the blender. "Don't knock it until you try it. The kids love it."

Maybe the kids needed a taste test. "Almond milk?"

"And it's far healthier than regular ice cream."

"Regular ice cream? Babe, they don't even print ice cream on the label. *Frozen dessert.*"

"Now wouldn't be the right time to work *babe* into the conversation, hot stuff." Teagan removed the lid from each container. "Besides, I prefer the coconut ice cream over regular stuff."

"Hmm," he grumbled, not believing that for a hot second. "You know the fat is what makes a steak taste good. No fat, bad steak. Probably stands true for ice cream."

"That's really gross if you think about it." Teagan stuck her tongue out. "Forget the fact that it's probably better for you. It tastes better."

Consider him unconvinced. "Explain to me what part of the almond was milked."

Teagan ignored him, popping off the lid of the peanut butter.

He chuckled. "I'm aware of how cows are milked. Eagle's Ridge High School did a so-so job of explaining how newborns are nursed." He winked. "Adequately enough that I could one day give the birds and the bees talk. If a certain someone ever let me."

She snickered, blushing.

"I could even walk us back every step, all the way to the

goat, if you placed a slice of goat cheese on a plate and asked how it was made." Noah picked up the almond milk container and shook his head. "But you've got me on this. Maybe I missed that day in biology."

Teagan turned for the silverware drawer and extracted a spoon. In one smooth move, she scooped a mouthful of chocolate almond milk frozen dessert and shoved it in his trap.

He laughed around the spoon, watching her more than he tasted what she tried to choke him with. Then he tasted it, and his smile doubled. "This is good."

"I know."

"I mean, really." Noah turned the spoon over and licked it. He wouldn't have known the difference between this treat and the real thing, and he reached for the coconut ice cream.

Teagan snapped her hand towel against his spoon. "No double dipping, good-looking."

"Ahhh, okay." Somehow he choked down his immediate response to argue for more ice cream and walked the few steps for another spoonful. Besides, they were all family and friends. Germs were germs. He got it. But they also shared a closeness that was like family, that deep connection that far surpassed any friendship he'd ever experienced. And the kids were like brother and sister even though they weren't, much as he and Lainey had been.

Noah tossed his used spoon into the sink as Teagan dumped the peanut butter into the blender. He dug out a scoop of the coconut ice cream. It was just as smooth and creamy as any other ice cream he'd had before. "This is good too. Maybe a little creamier."

"It's my favorite."

He tried to double dip again, and she swatted him away again.

Noah put his spoon in the sink. "Lainey used to make this for them?"

"She did." Teagan leaned against the counter, eyeing him with what he was sure was her school counselor assessment—kind and understanding while searching for what might lie underneath. "Lainey was one of the first in the medical field out here to bring the latest information to schools and doctors. Funny, nutrition isn't a part of many medical programs, and that was important to her."

Noah mumbled.

"She did a lot of good, Noah. Raised a great deal of awareness on many issues."

He crossed his arms. "A lot of good that did her. No microwave and nondairy ice cream." He wanted to be mad, but there was nothing but an empty sadness.

Teagan put the empty peanut butter container down and leaned against his chest. "She helped, and just because she was aware of many things, that doesn't mean she knew everything. Knowledge couldn't inoculate her against everything."

His chest hurt. A million ideas had been passed to him on how best to memorialize Lainey in the community. Some had suggested fundraisers while others tossed out the idea of an event like a gala or a fun run. Terrific ideas, but they weren't Lainey.

Noah had decided the best way to honor his cousin was to raise Bella as best he could. In a way that Lainey would have most wanted. He could do more good by sending another Lainey into the world than he could by raising a couple of thousand dollars.

Still it hurt. She helped everyone else and did everything right, except when she didn't, then Lainey didn't get a second chance.

Noah rested his chin on top of Teagan's head. "She had regrets. I don't know if she told that to anyone else."

Teagan shook her head. "No."

"She wouldn't have burdened anyone with that." He sucked in a deep breath. "That's who she was. Strong. A caretaker until she died."

"I know," Teagan whispered.

"She knew there was something wrong but ignored it until she couldn't pretend the symptoms weren't there."

Teagan cursed quietly.

"What does that leave us with? That she was stubborn, and it destroyed more than she saved?" She was a nurse, for crying out loud! Even if her cancer and symptoms were rare in her demographic, it still struck. Noah had fought many a night for sleep, wondering why she'd ignored symptoms of cancer that she could easily have diagnosed in men twice her age. But she was too young, too giving, to be an outlier.

Teagan shook her head. "Don't be angry at her. Please."

Maybe that was this feeling in his chest. "Why?"

"I don't know. Find a purpose in it, Noah. Or remember what she's given us. Love. Laughter. Bella."

His eyes burned. "True."

"Maybe there's more than even that. A greater gift that she imparted so her death isn't senseless."

"Like what?" His voice cracked.

"A lesson. Not to ignore the signs life gives us. That it doesn't matter when or how or why. There is no explaining a time line or its cause." Teagan wiped at her face. "You just accept it now or deal with that later."

Noah gathered Teagan in his arms, comforted by her warm hug and the wisdom in her words. He realized that what Teagan had said didn't apply only to health. Her words should be applied to life as well.

Noah wasn't just preparing Bella to be a little Lainey, ready to take on the world. He couldn't explain the intensity or quickness of it, but as he breathed in the familiar scent of her perfume, Noah knew he was holding his future.

He couldn't see the path. They hadn't even made it through dessert of their nondate dinner. But why deny what was there?

Noah kissed the top of her head again and gave Teagan a squeeze. "Our fake ice cream is going to melt."

She sniffled, laughing. "It's not fake, silly."

"Whatever it is, it tastes good."

As they stepped apart, Bella and Will wandered into the kitchen, their eyes drawn to the ingredients on the counter. Both went from calm to excited in two steps.

"Can we help?" Will asked.

Bella was already tugging a chair over. "We *can* help."

Amused, he let Teagan hop back to it as the kids took over the cartons and spatulas. They made short work of dumping the now-soupy frozen dessert into the blender.

"Take it easy." Teagan motioned with her hands to slow the rambunctious crew.

Noah stepped closer. They hadn't even had their milkshakes yet, and just the sight of the ingredients made Bella and Will hyper.

"Will, hang on," Teagan ordered as her son headed toward the wall with the plug.

Teagan held the blender's lid as she snaked Will off the counter.

Bella's pointer finger rose, and the room turned to slow motion as Noah reached for her. "Bella, wait—"

Too late.

The blender's whirl screamed a second before the cold splatter sprayed the room. Liquefied frozen chocolate slung across Noah's face, into his hair and covering his eyes.

Both kids screamed, turning into squeals, and Teagan's yell had joined them as both he and she raced to the blender, slapping it off.

Finally, the motor silenced. The whirling noise stopped. There was nothing but the quiet, heavy drip, drip, drip of coconut-and-almond-milk melted mess.

Noah swiped his face, glancing at Teagan. She was coated in chocolate. Her hair dripped with ice cream and small chunks of peanut butter. Every time Noah blinked, he had chocolate sludge stuck between his eyelashes.

No one made a sound as he wiped his face off again.

"Oh no," Will said quietly.

"We're sorry," Bella tacked on.

There was likely a section in every parenting resource that he'd ever read that dealt with this very situation. Teagan could likely write it.

A glob of chocolate fell from the ceiling, splattering onto the floor. He didn't move his face, but he let his eyes roam. The chocolate disaster was bad—but worse, or funnier, both kids were standing still like statues. Their arms were midmove, and milkshake dripped off them.

Soupy, liquefied chocolate dripped into the corners of his mouth. He fought the urge to lick his lips. Teagan shook her hands, and globs of peanut butter slipped off, *thwunking* on the wet floor.

His chest rumbled. He snorted, chocolate going up his nose.

Noah couldn't take it anymore. A plop of chocolate fell off a cabinet, landing between him and Teagan, then she shrieked, slapping her hands over her chocolate-covered mouth to hide the hilarity. Noah walked over to her, shaking his head, unable to keep a straight face. As nondates went, this one would go down in the record books.

"Eww, Will licked me," Bella cried out.

Then Noah lost it. He couldn't stop laughing. Teagan fell apart, pressing her dripping head to his chest, and he wrapped his arms around her.

When she took a breath, he took her sticky, wet hand. "Welcome to my life, *babe*. Can I use that word right now?"

"Yup, go ahead."

"If I can't live down the casserole, this one's on you."

Then it took everything he had not to kiss her.

CHAPTER TWENTY-TWO

THE MASTER BEDROOM would have anything that Teagan needed—including a shower—and Noah couldn't shake the laugh from his chest at the sight of her face when the blender exploded with the chocolate shake.

He might not live down the oven, but he'd certainly planned on teasing her about the dessert fiasco. Seemed fair. Cleanup duty had gone far beyond anything he'd anticipated.

"Hey, you." She quietly knocked on the bedroom door before walking in then rolled her eyes at herself. "Kids are asleep after I promised them *large* ice cream floats tomorrow."

"On one condition."

"Hmm?"

"I make them, and you're on cleanup duty."

She laughed. "Absolutely walked into that and will never live that down. Will I?"

"Yeah, I don't think so." He shook his head, trying to hide his laughter. Teagan's shirt and jeans were covered in smeared-dry chocolate ice cream.

"Don't laugh. You don't look much better."

He looked down, smirking. "I think your pants got the worst of it."

"But I'm pretty sure your hair's held up by sugar, not gel."

He leaned back, walked a couple of steps, and glanced in the mirror. *"Maybe* I missed a spot."

"Right here." She pointed. "And here." Laughing, she came closer and touched his ear and neck. "And here, and here—"

And he didn't care. Noah wrapped an arm around her waist, pulling her in front of him. They were finally alone, and he'd said a lot earlier in the store, a lot that he didn't know what to do with, but he did know that he was dying to get his mouth on her again. "I'm glad you're here."

Teagan nodded. "I am too."

Chocolate-scented air and sticky skin sounded like fun, but in reality, maybe not for tonight. Maybe it was a sign he needed to listen to. Something to tell him to put on the brakes.

Squeezing her close, he rested his chin on top of her head, hating that he was going to pull away from her. "Why don't you take a shower?"

He let go, grinding his molars when her fingers scraped against his sides.

"You don't want to go first?" she asked.

He wanted a million things having to do with that shower. But going first or second wasn't anywhere on the list.

"Towels are in here if you need more." He walked to the closet next to the bathroom. "And just make yourself comfortable. I don't really use this room much, anyway."

Teagan's eyes stayed on him while he pulled out a wash-cloth and tossed everything into the bathroom.

"Otherwise, you good?"

"I ruined tonight, didn't I?" she asked. "I don't know how you're used to things, but this probably isn't how you pictured anything."

Her standing in front of him, getting ready to shower. Yeah, it was how he pictured everything, actually. The fun. The family. The kids. All of it overwhelmed him in a way he couldn't explain, and that made him uncomfortable, but not with her. With what he might have missed out on, and what it took him to stumble into a missing link in his life. "You didn't ruin a thing, Teagan."

"I'm trying to read your mind, and my superpowers are failing me."

He crossed the room and took her hand, having no idea how to answer when he didn't understand how two people could collide in such a profound way. "Tonight's been one of those nights that makes me feel like the darkest hurt and the hardest challenges happen for a reason."

He didn't want to kiss her—didn't want her to think this was about stripping her naked and getting her in bed. Hell, he didn't know what he needed to do, so he spun her around to spend time with his words, and shower off.

They needed to get clean so they could get dirty. It was that simple. Standing here and talking was too emo heavy for him, especially when all he could think was that life sure came at you fast.

IF TEAGAN HADN'T been sure about the day's date, she'd have sworn she was hormonal. He nearly had her in tears on the way to the shower. Noah was being careful with her because of their kids, but she hadn't realized how much he was hurting because of Lainey. She should have known.

But she was a respite from that pain? It made her heart soar. Everything about him did, and for every foot higher that she climbed, she also found Noah immensely more attractive. Who knew that was possible? But the combination of a man with a heart and a rock-solid body had turned her into mush.

She ran the shower and quickly washed off the remaining chocolate from her skin and shampooed her hair. The soap smelled like him, and the steamy air swirled with a delicious need to be with him. *Physically.*

As the water beaded on her skin and the rivulets flowed off, she wondered how he would look in there with her too. Gah! She was finished and slapped the water off after taking perhaps the shortest shower of her life.

Rushing to dry off, Teagan didn't know what she would say. *Go get into the shower.* Or... She stepped out of the bathroom and faced a freshly showered Noah with a towel wrapped around his waist.

"Oh, hey. Thought I'd be out before you."

"I rushed," she said.

His grin hitched. "I'd say. You okay?"

"Very."

"Very," he repeated, and his playfulness heated. Noah tossed the T-shirt in his hand to the side.

He hadn't dried off the water droplets on his stomach and chest, and they followed the lines of his cut muscles. Teagan had known how thick his arms and shoulders were. Noah had held her against his torso, but as her eyes drifted toward the V hiding behind his towel, her mouth watered.

He prowled forward. Desire flared in his eyes with every bare step, and Teagan licked her lip as Noah tilted her chin up with the light touch of his hand. Shivers ran down her shoulders, cascading down her biceps. "Next time you're showering with me."

"Yes, please," she whispered.

"We can take our time."

Teagan nodded into his cupped hand, closing her eyes when Noah let his fingers drift across her skin and feather into her hair until he let the strands fall away.

"I like figuring this out with you. Having time with them, but then just you and me."

She didn't want to open her eyes. His fingertips drifted along her shoulders, and he said magical words. He took her hand in his and backed to the edge of the bed before sitting down. His thumbs massaged her wrist. Then he drew long strokes along her hand, up each finger, pulling one after the other. His thumbs worked her palm.

"That's *so...* nice." Unexpectedly erotic. He squeezed her hand and mimicked the same motions, massaging her wrists, running the length of her fingers, then putting pressure on her palms and working his way out, as though he knew each bone, every tendon and knuckle.

"Pressure points." He moved back to her right hand. "I'd always wondered."

"What?"

"The right place and touch can immobilize a person."

"Hmm." She believed it.

"But same place, different tactic." He brought her wrist to his mouth, and the heat of the wet kiss flamed through her body. Not just at her pulse point but awakening the nerve endings and heightening sensations until her core cried for his attention.

"Your experiment is working." A full body shiver slipped from her shoulders below her towel, and Noah languidly kissed up her forearm.

His lips paused, and he pulled her close, draping her arm around his neck. "Good to know."

Their two towels didn't hide much as he nestled her between his powerful legs. His palms drifted along her sides, pressing the shower-damp cloth to her flushed skin, and her pulse pounded in her neck.

Her towel-dried hair fell over her shoulders, and wet drips slid toward her breasts. Under the towel, her breasts ached for his touch, and even the tickle of water made her sizzle.

Noah's hands smoothed up her sides again, teasing along the top of her towel. His eyes held hers, and she waited for the rush of cool air when the towel fell away, but no.

He played. Tortured. He drew her closer again, dropping a hand to her backside and cupping her bottom while he skimmed the back of his knuckles over her covered breasts.

Her breaths shook. Her eyelashes fluttered. Still, the towel didn't move.

Noah squeezed her bottom, and Teagan's head dropped back on a throaty moan, and finally—

"Ah," she murmured.

His strong hand massaged her breast, and even through the towel, his focus on kneading her, working his way to the tip before sliding his hand to the other side, was heavenly.

He dipped forward, and hot breaths licked behind her ear as his fingers rested on the tucked knot of towel in the center of her chest.

"May I?" he whispered.

Arousal bloomed deep inside, and wordlessly she nodded.

Noah inched back, and with both hands, unwrapped her like a gift, baring her body to him as if he needed to feast. The towel dropped, and his hands did too. He took her fingers in his.

"I have never met anyone like you before, and damn, I'm glad."

Her heart squeezed. She was falling for him. Or she had already. It was fast. But it was deep. His presence consumed her. His honesty gave her life, and she inhaled deeply for fear that she'd let everything about this man overwhelm her. "Me too."

"On the bed, beautiful." He pulled her into the center of the king-sized bed.

"I'm not the only one." She tugged on the towel, and it fell off his hips so easily that she pulled back quickly, as if she'd made a move too fast. Her quick laugh stopped short at the sight of him naked and aroused.

Noah stole her breath. She couldn't keep from sliding her hands over his thickness, reveling in the smooth heat and the searing sound of his quick inhale. She didn't know pressure points, but she wanted him to feel as she did—blissfully beautiful and seductive. Sexy.

He made her feel like the center of his world, and stroking him, rubbing her thumbs along the top of his crown, she wished to give him that too.

CHAPTER TWENTY-THREE

NOAH DROPPED HIS head onto a pillow when Teagan slid her hands down him, but more than that, he needed her kiss. Her eyes. Her everything.

Easing back to her, he took her mouth, and their legs tangled. The kiss heated, and her body melted to his, arching for more with every gasping kiss and frenzied claw of her fingernails.

He ached to slide inside her. Every time she moaned, he wanted to make it louder, make it more, with deep thrusts and hungry kisses.

But—ugh—he needed to hold back. He'd specifically said no sex. None. God help him.

He didn't want to do Teagan. He wanted to be with her in a way he'd never needed before. Noah pulled back, needing to take a minute. He needed a plan. The don't-be-a-jackass plan. "Are you cold?"

Her face screwed. "*No.*"

"We should get under the covers." After all, who actually had sex with the covers on? He had no idea. But he didn't.

"Um…"

"Come on." Noah swallowed away every ounce of regret and made a to-do list. Worship her body, cuddle, cold shower. He tossed away pillows and yanked down the comforter. This was like staying in a hotel. No one ever had sex like this. Right?

It was a foolproof way to keep his word.

Her cute smile and wildly drying hair made him smile as she tucked under the blanket and sheet with him. "You didn't seem cold."

"I wasn't." He moved over her, and this didn't seem like a safer idea at all. If anything, they were closer than before, wrapped together in a way that he loved.

His plan was going off the rails, with her legs splayed under him and him towering over her, and they hadn't passed the five-second mark. It might've seemed that he was trying to move things along. Why did this have to be so complicated? And why did it matter?

Because he didn't want to lose her.

Recalibrate and stick to the plan. He shifted to her side and lowered his head to her breast, flicking his tongue over the tip and forgetting his worries when her back arched. That was his motivation. Make her feel him. Make Teagan fly, and he dipped his hands between her legs to find her wet and wanting.

"Noah," she whispered as he stroked her folds.

That gave him life. Her needy cries filled with his name. Selfish, but hell, he didn't care. His fingers parted her, encircling her rosebud of nerves before stroking her open and teasing her entrance.

"Like that." Her hips writhed. "Oh…"

He repositioned, kissing her mouth deeply as his fingers sank into her heat. Her muscles clenched, and his fingers withdrew from the slick tightness and plunged again. Teagan clung to him, kissing and moaning, promising she needed him.

His eyes squeezed shut, and he memorized her every breath and reaction. How she moaned and gasped, what made her arch and cry for more, until Teagan was on the cusp of climax and begging for his gaze.

He gave her that, pushing her over the edge, needing to watch as much as she did, and his chest exploded when her face tore away and the climax ripped through her.

Out of breath and intoxicated, he brought her to his body and wrapped her close as the last of her convulsions rolled through the limp woman in his arms. He kissed the top of her head and wondered if she would fall asleep. His heartbeat had dulled to a roar now, so maybe hers had too.

Noah shifted, and she wrapped her arms around his neck, nuzzling close. Like a spark to gasoline, his heartbeat galloped again.

"I thought you were asleep." He kissed her temple.

She sighed languidly. "I think that might've been a coma. But not asleep. At all."

Even her voice made his skin hot. It was time to bail. He stifled a groan and forced words out of his mouth. "You want me to wake you in the morning?"

She jerked, twisting from her sated position, and narrowed her gaze. "What?"

"Or not," he teased awkwardly. "I was going to let you sleep."

Teagan tensed, and her lips thinned into a smile he couldn't explain. "No, that's fine."

Fine. Lainey had warned him about the perils of *fine* years ago. Fine was a serious warning flag, and Noah had never given it a second thought. Until this second.

"You okay?"

"Sure."

He didn't recall *sure* being on the he-had-problems list, but he didn't know. Life on a SEAL team wasn't conducive to successful relationships, or so he'd heard. He hadn't had much interest in trying.

"As long as you're sure," he said.

Her eyes blinked more than he'd noticed before—did they look watery? In that moment, he knew. *Sure* could be classified the same as *fine* when a woman was upset, and he was about to be up shit creek, if he wasn't already there. Hadn't he just done a good thing?

"Hey." He dropped a kiss to her shoulder. "Teagan, look at me."

She glanced over for a moment.

"I hate to break it to you, beautiful."

Again she looked, but this time she didn't turn away. "What?"

"I have no idea what I'm doing."

Her eyebrows lifted as she scoffed, somewhat laughing. "I'll agree to disagree."

Noah laughed too and tucked her closer to his side. "Oh, *that*, I know."

She blushed, and he loved it, everything about her and them, how she reacted and how it made him feel, how she could react on such a base level and it would cause a seismic reaction within him.

"But not screwing up this?" He squeezed her side. "Because this is awesome? I don't know what the hell I'm doing."

"Seems okay to me," she said quietly.

"I invited you over for a nonsex slumber party, and here you are, naked, in bed with me."

Teagan shifted to her hip. "Because I want to be."

He worked that over for a second, staring at the ceiling. "Yeah, well, true."

"You're assuming." She sighed theatrically. "That I'm impervious to your charms? That I *just can't help myself* and need you to decide for me?"

He squinted an eye closed, chuckling at himself. "When you say it like that…"

"Oh, Casanova." Her shoulder-poking finger tapped with each syllable.

"I'm not going to live this down." He groaned.

"Hmm." Teagan leaned across his chest and planted a kiss on his lips. "We should keep a tally board."

He rolled her over and caged his forearms on the sides of her head. "Jokes aside, I said something, and I meant it. I invited you over because I would do about anything to spend time with you, and screwing that up was a concern of yours."

"Yours too," she added.

He shook his head. "Was. Everything was. I was in over my head, and there you were on the first day. Beautiful. A beacon of freaking knowledge, and maybe there was the off chance some primal instinct urged me to you because I needed you to survive. I'm trained to excel. But this isn't that. We're more."

"We are?"

"I know that. I just need you to also."

"I'm there." She hugged him, and the cold distance that had frozen her lips evaporated.

"Hang on a moment." Noah rolled out of bed, retrieved his wallet to remove a condom, and tossed the wallet on a nightstand. He was through with his plan and would let whatever happened between them happen.

Teagan had the covers pulled up to her chin then straddled him with the covers draped around her. Her wavy hair fell around his face when she kissed him. Their tongues slow danced.

Every deep kiss and velvety hot lick roared their smoldering fire to a blaze until her hips swayed and his arousal was a painstaking tease.

With few words shared, Noah removed the condom and covered himself. His hands gripped Teagan's hips. He sucked in a deep breath as she held him firmly against her tightness, inching down—and hovering—down—and waiting, until she took his length.

Her lips were parted, tiny quick gaps falling quickly, and never had he so wanted to lose control and stay in a moment forever.

Teagan rocked, and Noah didn't care anymore. His possessive hold took over, and her cries for more drove him to thrust. Their skin slapped together, their needs intertwining as she fell forward, her lips locking with his, and he folded his arms over her back and drove into her until she prayed to come again, then again.

He flipped her over, slowing as she pulsed around him, and embraced the racing need to be with her again. In bed. Out of bed. Then her eyes opened, and her sweet smile drifted to her lips, and Noah collapsed forward, nearly crushing her with his weight.

Their foreheads kissed. Their stomachs touched. He flexed in and out of her body as her mouth gaped out, another climax climbing through her, and this time, he'd go with her.

Sweat dampened his chest. He found her fingers, locking their hands together and straining. "*Teagan*."

She came with him, milking his release into eternity until he rolled them to their sides and gathered her in his arms.

CHAPTER TWENTY-FOUR

WRAPPED IN A security blanket of warm arms and heavy legs, Teagan stretched her naked body against Noah before silencing her cell phone alarm. She nestled back and didn't know if he woke with eyes that bright or if he'd been awake before her, but what a way to wake up.

"Good morning." His whiskery chin dipped to her cheek, and his chaste kiss was a shade quieter than his words had been.

His hands were sinfully slow as they slid over her, hugging her close, and her throat tightened as his lips tickled her with a delicious good morning kiss.

"Good morning to you too."

Noah shifted, tucking her close to his side, and Teagan snuggled her back to his chest as his broad body spooned her under the covers. He pulled her close one more time then let his hand rest on her bare hip, his fingers tracing patterns as she lulled in a dreamy happiness.

"What do you think our odds are?" he asked.

She tilted her head to see him better. "For?"

"Breakfast without a major malfunction."

"Ha!" She twisted to face him. "Maybe you're a kitchen jinx!"

"Nah." He kissed her. "Don't believe in jinx."

Her eyes rolled, and she kissed him back. "You better start, my friend. You are now living in the land of kids and dreams. That's *magic*."

"It'll be magic if we get out of bed before they wake up—"

Pfssh. "We're already up. No way are either of them going to see this hour."

"*Teagan*."

"What?"

"I said nothing about awake, beautiful."

She closed an eye and made a funny face, not deciphering his meaning.

"Out. Of. Bed." Noah rolled over her, teasing his lips across hers. "There's a distinct difference."

He proved his point with a kiss hot enough to make her dizzy. "I… get it."

His hands made fast work of moving everywhere, then he lumbered out of bed. "Having kids ain't easy."

She cracked up. "Says you with less than a month of time clocked."

He stopped cold then pivoted on his heel.

"I'm sorry." She sat up, sensing the immediate change in his mood. "I was just playing."

"This isn't a game to me, Teagan. I'm not going anywhere. I wouldn't do that to Bella."

The instant sting of what she'd implied sliced through her chest. "I know. Gosh, I didn't mean that—"

"And I wouldn't do that to you and Will. I'm not your ex-husband."

That pain flooded her eyes. They started to water. "I know."

He strode forward and pulled her to the edge of the bed. "Shit. Teagan."

"I'm sorry. I didn't—"

"I didn't mean to make you cry. Damn it."

"No, you didn't."

"You're crying. I was talking." He sat on the edge of the bed, and she crawled into his arms. "I overreacted."

"No. You didn't. Maybe I did. Or not." She wiped at her face.

"Hang on a sec." He moved to a drawer then tossed her a pair of boxers and an oversized shirt, then he pulled on a pair of sweatpants. "Try again. That whole thing about talking to a crowd when they're naked? It's bullshit. No one can think clearly like that."

Teagan laughed. "I think everyone has huge loads to carry. The older we get, the heavier our basket."

He nodded.

"And when couples do… coupley things, and their baskets are similar—"

"Are you sure you're a guidance counselor?"

She play-hit his arm. "Yes, to six-year-olds! I'm out of practice with grown-up issues."

"I could find a couple of dolls if you want them to have this conversation for us." He winked.

She smiled, disarmed, and he'd done what he'd intend-ed—as always. "You're good, I'll give you that."

"What?" Noah asked, pretending he hadn't just used some SEAL psych-ops tactic to put her at ease.

"I know enough to know you can disarm me."

He raised his eyebrows. "Maybe I just want to know what's on your mind. And maybe it hit me hard in the chest that I thought you compared me to your ex-husband who walked out on you. Both because I liked the idea of being your man and because I hated that you thought I could leave."

Teagan's lips parted. He'd stunned her. There was no

coming back from admissions like that. But she didn't want to. Her heart soared with possibilities and certainty that he was so much different than Spencer had ever been.

"I'm not saying rush anything," he continued. "But what I am saying is however this works out, it works out for the long term. Do you understand what I'm saying?"

God, she had no idea and too many ideas at once. Her stomach jumped into her throat. And just yesterday, she'd been wishing for one more kiss from him. "I think so."

"SEALs taught me not to predict the future, but they showed me something from very young."

"What's that?" she asked quietly.

"I always knew I was destined to be part of that team. I had no doubt. Just like Lainey had no doubt that I'd come home when it was time for me to re-up. She didn't waiver. She knew. Maybe it's in our genes. But that's the same as right now. I know."

"You know what, Noah?"

"That I'm supposed to be with you and Bella and Will, and that I'm falling in love with you."

CHAPTER TWENTY-FIVE

T HE GARAGE BAYS at Nuts and Bolts were lined with black silhouette cutouts of witches stirring cauldrons and of zombies with outstretched arms who were walking toward tilted graves. Noah's fingers were scrubbed clean, but pumpkin-orange acrylic paint had stained his close-cut fingernails. Maybe that would be his Halloween costume. Single dad, auto mechanic, *artiste*.

An old pickup rolled up and pulled Noah's attention from what had to be his greatest artistic feat. The door opened, and his old friend Ford Garrison jumped out.

"If I didn't see it with my own eyes, I would've called BS." He strode forward and stuck out his hand. "You're in town."

Noah did the same, shaking hands and embracing him with slaps on the back. "Good to see you, man."

"Not for long, and it's good to see you too."

They turned to survey all that Noah had put together for Nuts and Bolts.

"The witches' legs hanging out of that old charger"—Noah nodded toward the spot—"I think it's a nice touch. But not too much."

Ford cackled. "You've put a lot of thought into this. I'm really impressed."

Pride filled his chest in a much more distinct way than it had when serving his country. Both kinds brought him satisfaction, yet they met different needs. "What can I do for you? Something wrong with the pickup?"

Ford headed toward the stacked pumpkin-orange-painted tractor tires that overflowed with straw and decorations. Noah would use them as candy towers later, and he held out his hands, showing off fingernails stained the same colors as the tractor tires. "I'm not sure how long I'll have this orange reminder. But at least it's a good story."

Ford shook his head. "Did you forget how to use a paintbrush?"

Noah looked at the freshly healed scratches and Band-Aid–wrapped cuts. "Turns out there's only so much paper I can shred with an X-Acto knife before I get frustrated and start slicing."

"Do I even want to know?"

Noah chuckled, motioning for his buddy to follow. "Bella had a very specific person she is dressing up as for Halloween. Margaret Hamilton."

"Never heard of her."

"Yeah, me, either. That's a whole other conversation, but now I have, and the costume involves a nondescript dress, basic glasses, and…" They rounded the corner into Noah's office, and he held his arm out. "A couple of dozen reams of paper, hollowed out to reduce the weight and made to look like 1960s coding journals."

Noah gave his creation a tap, and the stacked books taller than Bella eased from his fingertips on the well-greased wheels attached to a base.

"You did all that overnight?" Ford asked.

Noah reached down to pick up the clear, high tensile line he'd attached to the base and secured throughout the tower. "I didn't realize how long it would take, but yeah, not too bad, if

I say so myself."

He gave the line a tug and handed it to Ford.

"Perfect weight distribution. And this is heavy enough that she could bring it along the parade route, but you hollowed it out?"

Noah nodded, letting a small amount of smugness scratch that. "Solid, right?"

"Dude, you realize what you've done, right?"

"Yeah, I built a badass prop for a badass historical figure that more people should know about."

"Tell me who she is in a second, but there will be a slew of mothers, and maybe fathers, who take this costume parade way too seriously and who will have you in their sites next year as a target to take out."

"Wouldn't be my toughest enemy." Noah snickered at the PTA-type drama that he planned to avoid at all costs. "And Margaret Lord Hamilton wrote the code for NASA that launched the Apollo."

"Bella came up with that?"

"Yeah, she did. I suggested a princess or a fairy."

Ford shook his head. "Sheesh, I wish you good luck. She's a helluva lot smarter than you."

Pride swelled in Noah's chest. "She is."

CHAPTER TWENTY-SIX

TEAGAN SLOWED HER Subaru into the parking lot at Nuts and Bolts. By the time she shifted into Park, she could almost feel Will exploding with energy for the Halloween parade. This year, she had allowed him to choose his own costume, and it ended up being a smorgasbord of all things scary and ghoulish.

Their plan was to meet Noah and Bella at Nuts and Bolts then walk to the start of the parade. From there, Teagan didn't know if Noah would head back to his shop or stick with them, but either way, her insides warmed at the thought of the community outing with him.

She and Will unbuckled, and her son waited impatiently for her to get out. Soon as her hand rested on the door lever, he split.

"I'll be with Bella."

Teagan smiled as she caught sight of Bella stepping from the office entryway. Her costume was spot-on. The 1960s A-line dress was of period-piece quality, and Teagan wondered where Noah had come up with such a pint-sized look.

Bella's glasses were just like the picture Teagan had sent to Noah, but it was the straight-ironed brown hair that Bella wore with the dated outfit—including the tights and strapped Mary Janes—that completed her very serious look.

Will ran across the parking lot, still in normal clothes, and

Teagan reached into the backseat for the large bag filled with random Halloween accessories that would become his costume. Then she grabbed her purse and backpack and followed the kids inside, taking in the fantastic job Noah had done with the backlit silhouette scenery and tire towers painted pumpkin orange.

When she walked inside, she half expected just as much effort put into the over-the-top decorations, but Noah had simply covered the waiting area and hallway with a gauzy spiderweb that reached every corner and worked its way down the hallway and over the front counter.

It was perfect.

Nuts and Bolts had its own personality already with a clock made out of wrenches and license-plate lampshades. Adding anything else would have been too much. Sometimes, Teagan wondered if Noah knew that he had such a killer instinct.

Noah was dressed as an astronaut in a gray suit, with an American flag and Apollo patch on his sleeve and a helmet over his head. As he walked down the hall, Teagan couldn't wipe away her smile.

He wasn't just an astronaut. He was Margaret Hamilton's astronaut because that was not a modern costume. The helmet looked older and likely matched the late 1960s and early 1970s launches she influenced. Same with the suit. Teagan clapped as he came closer.

"If you two do not win the Halloween costume contest, I call foul." She walked up to him, and Noah removed his helmet.

"Hey, beautiful." He wrapped an arm around her waist and gave as chaste of a kiss as they could manage with the kids nearby. "I love your costume too."

"What are you talking about?" She made a face, inspecting the clothes she'd had on all day. The black leggings and Halloween-inspired shirt were in no way a costume. At least, she hoped.

"I don't know, it looks like you're dressed up as a miracle worker or…" He put his hands on her shoulders and held her out, moving her side to side as though inspecting. "I'd say a model, but that doesn't seem like your type of costume. You're damn gorgeous, though. Maybe a—"

Teagan wrapped her arms around him, pulling Noah back for another kiss that was less chaste than they're not-so-chaste kiss before.

"Mom," Will called from the front of the shop. "I need help with my costume."

She drew back, letting her hands slide down the front of Noah's chest. "Halloween duty calls."

"Oh, I know what you're dressed as. That lady they make all those magnets and mugs for."

She turned around while walking away. "What lady?"

"The world's greatest mom." He winked then donned his astronaut helmet.

Teagan could've used a helmet of her own to mask what had to be the gooeyness that melted across her. If he wasn't melting her with a kiss, the man was stealing her heart. She had no idea that his complimenting her parenting would be as endearing as it was intoxicating. Nor did she know that the little things, details like his matching costume and antiquated astronaut helmet, would cause her heart to latch onto his.

It was one thing to swoon over a Navy SEAL who could play with a toddler or hold a baby. An image like that was sure to make anyone's heart pound.

But a tough guy like Noah, so far out of his league and

doing whatever it took for a young girl who didn't fit into the category of normal? There were easier ways to do what he was doing, and truthfully, Bella wouldn't have noticed the difference. Teagan never would've known; the day would've gone fine.

But he really cared. And so did she—about him, for him, and for them. He made it so easy to fall in love.

CHAPTER TWENTY-SEVEN

WILL WALKED THROUGH the empty garage bay, wearing what Noah could only describe as everything. A cape hung down his back, and a panel of lights and gadgets lit up his chest. He had the leg of a werewolf but the shield of a superhero and the baton of a space galaxy defender. His wizard hat rested crookedly on top of a ghoul's mask.

"Will, that is, by far, the most clever costume I've seen," Noah said.

Bella whirled around to inspect her friend then turned to Noah, pulling behind her the stack of books that easily bested her by several inches. "I thought you said I would be the smartest recreation."

He stepped forward and wondered if one day, Bella would do something as great as Margaret Hamilton had done. No doubt she would. "There's a difference between clever and smart, and categorically, the two of you are in vastly different costumes."

Bella's head tilted as though she were funneling the definitions of *clever* and *smart* through her brain, then Will bopped her on the head with his glowing baton.

"Categorically," she said, "we are different, but the same level of smart and clever."

Noah nodded, agreeing because sometimes that was best with a woman, or girl, with arguments he didn't completely understand and that had no long-term repercussions. At least, that was what he decided on the fly. "Sounds good, ladybug."

Will and Bella simultaneously cried out that she wasn't a ladybug, as if they'd never heard his nickname for her before. On that note, Noah took his astronaut helmet and put it on his head, having nothing redeeming to offer to the conversation, and Bella turned as the bathroom door opened and Teagan emerged.

Her skirt was long and flowing, as was the gauzy white shirt that clung to her figure. Necklaces gathered down the center of her shirt, and slender chain belts wrapped around her waist, dangling off her hips in a way that caught his eye, mesmerizing him with her every step. She clinked and jingled, as though soft bells played as she walked, and her wrists were decorated in bangle bracelets. Teagan had tied back her thick hair with a brightly woven scarf, and Noah had no word for her costume except *entrancing*.

"Do you like?" Teagan spun. Her skirt flared, and the jewelry jangled.

He loved it far more than he would admit in front of the kids. "Yup, but what are you? A pirate?" He had no idea.

She pulled out the skirt, and her jewelry clinked. "Hmm. You're in the right neighborhood."

"Spin again," Bella cooed, seemingly enamored with the flowing skirt and colors.

Teagan took a handful of her skirt, held it out, and swayed her hips side to side as they all laughed and enjoyed her costume. "Any guesses? I'm not a pirate, and it might have something to do with work. Or at least people chattering with me at work."

"You're Hildie," Noah announced.

Teagan's costume fit the bill. Brightly colored, check.

Would scare Zane's dog, check. Liked chatter, major check.

She tipped back and howled. "That may be the funniest, most Eagle's Ridge thing you have ever said." But Teagan righted herself, giving him a quick headshake. "But no." She turned to Will and Bella. "Please don't repeat what Noah just said."

Oh yeah. Whoops. He'd never live that down. "Let's keep those lips zipped. Please."

Neither kid seemed clued in, and they agreed.

Teagan wriggled her jewelry again. "I'm a psychic! Don't I look like those ladies who show up on late night commercials?"

Both kids took turns jumping up and down and calling out "You do, you do."

Noah's confused glance at them didn't slow down their reaction. He was positive neither had seen a middle-of-the-night television commercial.

Teagan wryly twisted her lips. "So many parents assume I can predict the future that I thought a little bit of school counselor humor would be fun."

"I love it," he said.

"It'll be lost on the people who might be offended." She crossed her fingers. "I hope."

There wasn't anything about Teagan he didn't adore. Even the way she worried about the people who drove her crazy. Noah walked toward his grinning psychic and took her hand in his. "Time to go?"

"Yes! It's time! Can we go now?" Will asked. "Please!"

"Please?" Bella pulled her stack of books toward the front door. "I think it already started without us."

"It didn't," Noah said.

The kids weren't sold on that answer and peered out as though they could see through the dark and down the block to the start of the parade. He leaned close to Teagan. "What, pray tell, does this psychic foresee in the near future?"

Her fingers intertwined with his as they ambled behind the kids. "A long walk for me in the dark with two awesome kids and then a long night for the two of us warming up."

"Is that what you think?" She didn't know he planned on walking with the three of them. Nuts and Bolts used to hand out candy to the parade goers and people along the sidewalk. Hell, Teagan was the one who reminded him. But there was no way they were walking in that parade without him. He squeezed her hand tight. "Wait outside for me. I'll be there in a minute."

Will and Bella were already outside and racing around, Will chasing Bella's books on wheels, and Teagan pressed up on her toes to kiss his cheek. "Sure thing."

Then Noah walked behind the counter and pulled out two large buckets full of candy, stacked one on top of the other, and took his keys and cell phone from a shelf. He slipped them into one of the pockets of his astronaut costume.

He lifted the heavy containers of candy and pushed out the front door of Nuts and Bolts, surprising Teagan.

"What are you doing?" she asked.

"Get ready." He made way to the first orange tower of tractor tires and dropped the heavy container of candy to the ground.

Teagan stepped closer. "For what?"

He hoisted the first bucket, wondering how many pounds of chocolate, licorice, suckers, and taffy it took to fill each, and placed it on top of the straw-covered tower. Then he grabbed the second one, carried it to the other side of the parking lot entrance, and did the same in the other tractor tire tower he'd made to hold the candy.

Noah dusted off his hands and looked at the two tire towers, topped with enormous buckets of candy. "That'll do the trick."

"Are you kidding me?" Her excitement made his orange-painted fingernails worth it.

"Nope." Noah space-walked to the sound of the kids' laughter toward the side of the shop where he'd painted "Help yourself" on the front of two rusted-out, abandoned car hoods. He moved each one to stand by a tire tower, securing them with the metal poles he'd attached.

Teagan jingled and clinked her way to meet him in front of Nuts and Bolts, and he hooked his arm around her. "I don't know about you, but I think it gets the point across."

"I can't believe it." She laid her head against his astronaut arm. "You're not staying here?"

He kissed the top of her head. "You're going to have to work on your fortune-telling if you want to be the Eagle's Ridge psychic. Because I'm walking with you all night long. And I'll be up with you tonight too. *All night long.*"

She swung in front of him so that their torsos touched, and her smile was sweeter than any of the sugar he had put out.

"Is Teagan your girlfriend?" Bella called from across the parking lot.

A grin cracked on his face, and he chuckled at their pint-sized audience and the commentary. There was no use trying to tell Bella that Teagan was his world because Bella would take him literally, and they'd never make it to the Halloween parade if Noah had to explain that he understood that Teagan was a person and not a planet. Nothing like a five-year-old who was smart as hell except when the topic wasn't quite at her level yet. "I don't know, Teagan. How do you feel about titles? Are you my girlfriend?"

She tipped her head, tapping a finger against her chin. "Hmmm. I do collect them."

"I should have realized that." He took her thought-pondering finger and counted off, "Mom. Counselor. Psychic. Girlfriend."

Teagan's eyes lit. "*Girlfriend.*"

They needed a candy apple or whatever the Halloween equivalent was for mistletoe because he had run out of excuses for randomly kissing, but oh well. Noah kissed his girlfriend only to receive cheers from Bella and Will.

Teagan ducked her head, giggling quietly, then turned against him as he wrapped her to his chest. "Well, that's a first."

"Let me go get my helmet and lock up."

As Noah walked by Bella and Will, he laughed as he heard their whispers.

"Noah?" Will ran up to him.

"Yeah, buddy?"

"Thank you."

He stopped. "What for?"

"Even though it's Halloween, you make people smile. Even when it's not Halloween. Like Bella and my mom." Will ran back to Bella, not knowing what his words might've meant to Noah.

"Thank you too, kid," Noah said quietly. For all the classified ops and the good they'd done around the world, never once had a single mission made him feel as that kid just had. He was where he was supposed to be.

CHAPTER TWENTY-EIGHT

KIDS IN COSTUME and their in-costume parents walked the Main Street route waving to the community who brought candy and tossed it from the sidewalk as they walked by. The Eagle's Ridge tradition was a slight twist on trick or treating, replacing the door to door knocking. It brought families out from both sides of town, and added that little touch of specialness that the community thrived on.

Teagan shivered and curled under Noah's astronaut arm as they walked behind Bella and Will who ran from one side of the street to the other with a group of their friends, showing off their costumes and snatching thrown pieces of candy. "Can you see through that thing?"

His helmet-covered head tilted toward her. "What?"

"Can you," she raised her voice, then stopped. Obviously, he couldn't.

Noah pulled off his helmet. "Just kidding, I could hear you fine. But I'm fogging up."

She snickered but then burrowed into him. "I'm cold, even with long johns under my outfit and heating packs tucked everywhere that they'd hold."

He pulled her close, and she snuggled against him, enjoying the festivities.

"Hang on a sec." Noah gave her a quick squeeze and stepped away.

She followed his gaze toward one of the Eagle's Ridge police officers who had them in his sights. The man's tight face was pinched and locked on Noah, even as the astronaut separated from the parade and moved closer.

Will fell back. "Where's Noah going?"

"Just to talk with a friend."

"His friends are the police?"

She nodded and her jewelry clinked as they continued to walk in the parade. "Sure. He has all kinds of friends. Just like you do."

"It's good that he's a good guy." Will spun away.

Amused, Teagan watched her son run back to his group of friends then walk with Bella. "It's good, that's for sure."

Bella and her rolling tower of books stopped with Will, and Teagan continued to walk in the parade. The kids started walking again when she reached them.

"If Noah is a good guy, would that make him like a prince?" Bella asked.

Teagan tried to understand the basis of her question. "I'm not sure I understand."

"You could be a princess and he could be a prince. Then you both could match."

She held her bangled wrists out. "But I really liked being a fortune-telling gypsy, so that wouldn't have worked."

Bella and Will scowled, and Will asked, "Are you sure?"

Her smile cracked. "Yup. Positive. And I'm also positive Noah wanted to be an astronaut."

"Really?" Bella's nose scrunched. "Are you sure?"

Teagan pressed her lips together. "You can ask him. But he chose his costume."

They trotted again, conversing with their heads together, then dropped back again. Bella asked, "What are you going to be next year? A princess?"

"I'm not sure."

"You should be. And he could be a prince."

Will nodded, swinging his bag of candy. "Because they go together."

"I don't know. We'll see."

Bella tossed her head back and scowled, but then ran after a handful of thrown candy. Will gave Teagan a placating grin. "That wasn't what she thought you'd say."

"I could tell," she laughed.

"But we can still make it work."

Teagan had no idea what they were talking about. "All right, baby. You do that. Go have fun."

Whatever Bella had in mind, Teagan had a feeling that it had to do with her favorite movie prince and princess that kissed at the end. "Very cute."

Noah walked back over, eyeing her. "Did I just see you talking to yourself."

"Bella has our costumes picked for next year. *We're matching.*"

He chuckled. "I can't wait."

"I bet." She nodded to the direction he'd come from. "What was that all about?"

"Eagle's Ridge PD had a report of suspicious activity in your neighborhood, and they went to check it out."

"Really?" Someone else had their shed shredded?

He shifted his helmet from one arm to the other and tucked her under his arm. "Someone parked a van a block away from your house and it 'didn't look right' according to a neighbor. So they parked a car on your street for a while. Nothing came of it."

"The wild crime in Eagle's Ridge."

"Nothing to complain about," Noah said.

"That's the truth." Perfect place to raise a family and live their lives. Everything was easy—or would be. She'd convinced Noah to spend time at Lainey's grave, and that would be heart wrenching. But after that, if they could all survive that, they could do anything.

CHAPTER TWENTY-NINE

T HE OLD CEMETERY wasn't old by East Coast standards. Still, Noah pulled down the winding road with his wrist draped over the steering wheel as though he hadn't a concern. He couldn't help being glad that Teagan sat shotgun.

His mom had told him that Bella would do fine. His dad said the same thing but not in so many words. Taking Bella to Lainey's gravesite wasn't Noah's concern. He hadn't been there since the funeral. He was the concern.

It was more than the weight of losing the woman who might as well have been his sister. They had been raised just as his mom and uncle were, as twins. At times, when Noah and Lainey were kids, they'd believed that they defied logic and science and were also somehow twins.

The small church served most everyone in the community, and they passed it, rolling by on their way to the church's lot. He pulled the dually truck into an unmarked space and shifted into Park. Both kids were unusually quiet, and the slide of the gearshift clicked loudly in the cab. Noah sighed, resting his elbow on the center console. Teagan cupped her hand over his in the silence.

"Are we ready to go see them now?" Bella asked from the backseat, sounding more chipper than sad.

He honestly didn't expect it to be this hard. Not trusting his voice, he nodded, and Teagan squeezed his hand, opening her door first.

"Of course, sweet pea. Let's get you guys unbuckled."

Her door shut, and she let both kids out of their restraints. Then they burst, if not respectfully, toward where Lainey and her husband lay buried. Noah hadn't even unbuckled.

Teagan ducked her head through the door that the kids had exited. "Doing okay?"

He held her eyes but shook his head. "This isn't fair for them."

Teagan shut the kids' door and walked to his but didn't open it, standing there until he opened it himself. When Noah pushed out, he eased his arm over her shoulder. She tucked against the crook of his arm and hooked a thumb into his belt loop.

They followed the trail that the kids had made, passing row after row of pristine gravesites scattered with flowers and flags, many traditional stones, and others adorned with crosses and testaments to patriotic duty.

They summited a small hill to see both kids cross-legged in front of the Force plots. Bella's little mouth and hands were moving a mile a minute, as though she were explaining to her parents everything that had gone on since she last saw them. Will ran his hands over the grass beside her while she did. Noah expected Bella to sob, but instead it was more like a regularly scheduled update with her mom. His throat burned as he tried to understand.

"Bella's doing very well. Considering," Teagan said quietly.

"Yeah, she is. But I don't get it. Why that little ladybug has to go without Lainey and Davis. I'd be shattered."

"She is." Teagan paused. "And in our own ways, we are too. But we take those devastated pieces, patch them together, and you'll see life's a mosaic. It's not fair. It's unforgiving. It steals the unflawed and the innocent, but we can take what's broken and build a beautiful life that we never saw coming and, now, can't live without."

There were times over his military career when his team had lost men and women who didn't deserve their fate. Families were robbed of their loved ones and their future full of memories. Noah wished he could go back in time and share Teagan's words with them. How did one woman comprehend what he had felt many times before but been unable to name or understand? He still didn't understand but maybe was inching toward acceptance.

"I'm really glad you're here." He clung to Teagan's hand as they proceeded closer.

Bella was finished with her enthusiastic conversation, and after a couple of giggling glances at Noah and Teagan's handholding, both kids settled into a secretive conversation, lying on their stomachs until they rolled onto their backs and stared at the clouds.

What was he supposed to do at a gravesite? Noah had never understood that. At least, he didn't know what someone was supposed to do there for extended periods of time. If there had been a fallen SEAL or anyone he'd fought alongside, he had lowered his head and said a few words. That he would continue their fight and protect their loved ones. That their effort was not for a lost cause and their death had a purpose.

He didn't understand Lainey's death. That death had a purpose that eluded him.

"Look!" Will pointed toward the sky. "A shooting star!"

"Where? Where?" Bella searched frantically.

"Right there." Will pointed.

"That's an airplane. It's too slow."

"No it's not," Will snapped.

"Quick, make the wish, make the wish!"

"I'm making the wish!"

"Will, Bella," Teagan hushed them. "Too loud. Take it down a couple notches."

Noah had to laugh at Bella and Will's frenetic wish making, despite Teagan shushing them. Maybe that passing airplane was Lainey intervening with a moment of laughter and love because she wouldn't want him spiraling into depression over her death, not that Noah listened very well.

He scrubbed his hands over his face. He never listened. Not back in high school when Noah got into a fight with Jack, after Noah assumed his buddy had dumped Lainey. Nope, she'd dumped him. And he didn't listen when she said she was dying. Noah's first response had been denial as he kept looking into cancer treatment options that her medical team hadn't thought about.

He made a mental note to drop Jack a phone call. Jack hadn't turned up for Lainey's funeral, and that had thrown Noah for a loop. He wasn't sure how to feel about Jack.

"Everything okay?" Her slight eyebrow lift indicated that her concern was far greater than the delicate wording of her question.

"Just thinking about an old friend of Lainey's." Noah cleared his throat. "And in general, how I wanted to protect her from everything, and in the end couldn't... From anything."

"You've seen worse than I have." Teagan leaned against him. "With life and loss. Devastation. So you know life's not fair."

His throat continued to tighten, and his eyes burned. He shut them and faced the sun. "Yup."

"No one lives to the last chapter of their book like we want them to. But her book didn't end, because it's a story. Bella's living it. You're living it."

Eyes still closed, he squeezed Teagan's hand in silence.

"Everything hurts because you're paging through the past right now. Which you should do." She squeezed back then relaxed. "But you're wishing there were more of Lainey in the next pages without realizing that there absolutely is."

He glanced down, his gaze sun-bleached. "How so?"

"Grieve, Noah, because grief never goes away until it's ready, but treat it like unspent love that's collecting in the form of pain and unshed tears. You're keeping it to yourself, but whether you realize it or not, you've found a way to lavish that in the form of love on that little girl who feels the same way you do."

He dropped his gaze to the kids and back to her, then he looked over the horizon, past the church, over the green landscape of Washington State trees fed by powerful rivers and a community of good people. What was he doing? Remembering everything that he'd had growing up. Patient conversations. Meaningful moments. He was always with his cousin and extended family and those who made him feel confident and cared for—all similar to how he was raising Bella, just as her mother had.

Noah had already told Teagan his intention for the long term, but not until that moment did he understand the gravity of what that meant—family.

This was his story. Eagle's Ridge was how it all came together, and Lainey and Davis's tragedy wouldn't end there. Exactly the way Lainey would want.

CHAPTER THIRTY

TEAGAN GATHERED THE kids. Their attention spans had long flittered away, and she held Will and Bella in each hand so they could go for a short walk and leave Noah for a few minutes. Kids were resilient and terribly honest, and she didn't know if they would have questions about life after death or maybe why she and Noah were holding hands.

Over the years, Teagan had advised plenty of parents on this very topic. The question of introducing new relationships to kids was one that had to be handled with care. Adults could easily have many friends. But kids of all ages noticed special friendships and relationships, when they started and if they ended, and how they were handled and how they were communicated best determined how well a child reacted.

She and Noah hadn't said much, but they had been honest.

Still, there might be questions. With Bella, there were always questions or a comment more suited for an adult.

"Why don't we have a Thanksgiving parade?" Will asked.

"Yes, how come? We could have the balloons go down Main Street."

Teagan laughed. She was so focused on serious topics that the wave of relief that washed over her nearly made her woozy as they bantered back and forth about the need for another major Eagle's Ridge community event. "We just had the

Halloween parade, you two. I don't think I could handle another extravaganza."

Will tugged on her arm. "You could hold the string so the hot air balloons don't fly away." He swung one way and Bella the other. "And that way Santa would have to come at the end of the parade, and we would all get to talk to him."

Bella froze as though she'd just realized the perfect gift to ask for, her eyes wide and her mouth open, then she jumped in the air with Teagan's hand still knotted to hers. "Yes! We need a parade."

"Don't be silly," Teagan said. "We will see Santa, with or without a parade. You know that."

"But we need to see him now," Bella pleaded as Teagan looped them around and headed back toward Noah. "Let's make it through Thanksgiving before we talk about any other holiday." She squeezed both of their hands and spun them in a circle. "Deal?"

Both kids chimed in with their agreement as Noah strode forward and met them, and Bella took off to jump into his arms.

He tossed her over his shoulder as if she was his Nuts and Bolts bag then ruffled Will's hair. Her son roared, darting ahead, and Noah hooked his arm around her. Such an odd location to find a peaceful moment, but as they walked back toward his dually, Teagan listened to their laughter as the cool breeze lifted her hair, and she knew all was right in her world.

"How about we meet back up for an early dinner?" Noah asked as they pulled out of the church driveway.

"Hey, Mom?" Will mumbled, half talking to Bella also.

"Oh, that's a great idea," Teagan told Noah. "I actually want to try this new dish with butternut squash and pine nuts. If you drop us off at the organic market, I think they'll have everything that I'll need."

"Can I show Bella that game on your phone?" Will followed up.

"We'll wait, or go in with you," Noah said.

"I have to use the restroom. And I'd rather use *my* bathroom. Can we go there first?" Bella asked. "I have to go very badly."

"Can I show Bella now?" Will asked again.

Teagan fished her phone out of her purse and handed it to Will. *Very badly* were bathroom code words she didn't like to hear, so she was up for anything to use as a distraction. "Sure. Here." She handed it to Will then faced Noah. "Drop us on the way, and you two go straight home. No biggie. We'll see you soon enough."

"Thank you," Bella said in a very petite, very adult way over the sound of the game in Will's hand. "I appreciate that."

"Sure thing," Teagan said.

Noah smiled. "Then we'll just swing back and pick you up."

"I'll be so fast in the store, you don't need to. The walk and the fresh air?" She shrugged. "We can hoof it, no problem."

They crossed Sentinel Bridge, made their way down the street, and pulled in front of the market. She leaned over and kissed Noah on the cheek, feeling a blush rise to her cheeks as his innocent looking hug gripped her tightly, then she let Will out and they waved goodbye.

It took only a few moments to find the pine nuts and butternut squash and then check out. Walking down the street, swinging the heavy bag between them, Will asked, "Are you sure that you like kissing Noah?"

She blushed, caught off guard by the directness and timing. "I'm sure. I like him a lot. And thank you for checking."

They continued down the block as Will explained fun facts

about dung beetles, but she circled back to his kissing question. "Hey, sweet pea. Are you okay that I kissed Noah on the cheek?"

It wasn't the first time she'd asked him that type of question, though maybe she hadn't opened the conversation like that before. But she and Noah had already talked to both kids ad nauseum, just to be sure, though a couple of their follow-ups had been scripted, intentionally indirect and super sly.

"Sure," Will said. "I just want to make sure that you're happy before we do something that we shouldn't."

Be still my heart. She melted into a puddle of mush and dropped to her knees, pulling him into a hug. She couldn't love Will any more for grouping him and her together into a *we*. All of their conversations had paid off, and he understood that she'd move forward with a relationship only if he was on board.

A million factors were in play, and all of them revolved around him. But that he referenced *we*, as though they were the ones pulling the strings for the relationship with Noah, really hit her in the feels. "You make me so proud. Thanks for looking out for your mama."

She stood up and let him wriggle away, changing the conversation back to dung beetles and mealworms. Will trotted ahead, and she floated for the rest of the walk home.

They came onto their block and arrived at their house. He waited impatiently as she searched for her keys, and once the door was unlocked, Will burst inside and Teagan stepped in, dropping her grocery bag and purse while kicking off her shoes. She glided into the front hall on cloud nine, pausing at an unfamiliar stench of… dirt and tobacco.

"Who're you?" Will's surprised voice faintly called from the hallway upstairs.

And Teagan's blood ran cold.

CHAPTER THIRTY-ONE

"WILL!" TEAGAN RUSHED up the stairs. "Will!" she sputtered, tripping over herself to pull her son behind her as she stared at the end of the hallway. "Spencer? What are you doing in here?"

"Spencer?" Will repeated, now more curious than scared. He knew his father's name. He peeked around her. "Is that—"

"Hold on." She pushed Will behind her, backing them both against the wall as two other men stepped out of the hallway bathroom. They stank of cigarettes and sweat, along with something else. A fine dust tickled her nose, tinged with the scent of home repairs, and Teagan studied one man who was covered in white dust. "Will, go downstairs." She walked them along the wall, hanging onto Will. "Go next door and play with—"

Voices and boots coming from her kitchen stopped her cold.

At the base of the stairs, a new man stopped midstep as he saw her at the top of the landing.

"Who are these guys?" Will's whisper shook because even a five-year-old could sense evil.

"They're just friends of a friend," she said lightly, turning back to Spencer. "My old friend stopped by with his friends."

Her light tone did nothing to ease the aggressive nature of the men surrounding them, and she silently pleaded with

Spencer.

"Why are they here?" Will pushed.

"Spence?" Teagan bugged her eyes.

"Looking for something?" a man with a cigarette tucked behind his ear offered.

"Right." Teagan swallowed against her dry throat. "I'd be happy to help. Could we do this in a less invasive manner?"

He shook his head.

Spencer didn't give so much as a long look at Will, who tugged her shirt. "Is that my dad?"

"Um, I—" She had no clue how to handle this real-life unfolding disaster. "We'll figure out who everyone is soon enough." She straightened and glared at Spencer with every ounce of anger that she could launch his way. "Can Will go next door and play? *Please.*"

Her ex-husband shook his head. "He can stay put until we have what we need."

"And that is?" she prompted, finding a whole new level of eyeball anger to level at Spencer.

"I allowed a business partner to store a few things for safekeeping before we—er, anyone moved in, and, well…" Spencer shrugged. "He owed my *friends* here a great deal of money. Plus interest, and we're here to recoup."

"A few things for…?" She blinked, unable to spit the words back at him. "Well, get them and go."

"I don't know where exactly he stashed them." He squinted. "And since he's no longer *with us*, I can't ask. Otherwise, we would've split ten minutes after you took off. I'd been trying to do this with less theatrics, but apparently the time for that search method has passed."

Her teeth sealed. "Well, *thank you.*" Teagan couldn't have pried her molars apart for a pleasant conversation if she had to, and she growled the rest. "For trying to be considerate."

"No longer with us." The other man behind Spencer gave a good snort.

"You think this is funny?" she snapped. Maybe she didn't have lockjaw after all as she failed to see the humor in breaking and entering then joking about murder in front of Will, even if he was too young to read between the lines.

"Easy, Teagan. No one else needs to get themselves killed," Spencer said.

She swung toward him. "*What? Me?*"

"The diamonds are *worth* more than you. Don't slow them down." He glanced at her vents thoughtfully. "They're in the walls somewhere. We've found some, but not all, and none were where I thought they'd be."

"Diamonds?" she shrieked. Spencer had never told her! Wasn't that the entire point of his treasure hunting career?

"*Blood* diamonds."

Oh, God. "In my house?"

He lifted a shoulder. "They were an investment. We'd grab it when we needed them, and now, babe. I need them now."

She couldn't take it anymore. "Get out of my house!"

"Yeah, it's not going to work like that." He motioned behind him to the man with a sway back. "Some friends are pushier than others."

The man at the base of the steps took a heavy step up.

Tension stormed in her chest as Will fidgeted by her side. "Let's find what you need to, and you can be on your merry way."

"Tea, don't be a bitch."

The pressure in her head was too much. Teagan was going to explode. She should be scared, but instead it was white-hot fury like she'd never experienced before. The audacity! For him to call her a name! In front of her child! She shrieked, her hands balled into fists. "Don't break into my house!"

Spencer laughed. "Used to be ours, and I was more than fair to you in the terms of our divorce. All I needed was access. I just need it earlier than I realized, babe."

Babe? "Get out!"

"Mom?" Will touched her back. "What if they kill him?"

Teagan's breath came in pants, and she needed to calm down, not wanting to say anything in front of Will that she'd regret. "He can sit in his room, and I'll help you find whatever you want. Deal?"

Spencer turned to the other men then asked, "He got an iPad or anything?"

"*Can I* have an iPad?" Will jumped to life, not realizing the gravity of the situation.

The men laughed, and Teagan wanted to throat punch them one by one. "Go to your room, baby. I'll check on you soon."

As though he didn't understand that thugs—or whoever Spencer was in a bind with—were standing in the way, Will politely said "Excuse me" as he slipped past and into his room.

"Nice kid," the other man said. "My old lady's all the time on our rug rat about 'cuse me."

What world was she living in where criminals were complimenting her kid's manners? "Thanks."

Spencer brushed by and walked toward the master. "Maybe it was the bedroom and we missed it."

"I can go downstairs and check for something. Just tell me where." And maybe that would be by her phone, so she could call 9-1-1 and then Noah." Why hadn't she kept her purse on her shoulder!

The other man came up the stairs. "You can stick with us."

"I prefer you to leave, if we're being honest."

"We'd prefer your old man didn't steal from us. But that's life."

Her heart stalled. "*You stole* from them?"

"Semantics," Spencer said, downplaying. "Can we focus?"

She walked into the bedroom. "Oh my…" The walls were sliced open. The wallpaper had been shredded. The vents were unscrewed and torn away, and the light fixtures were ripped down. "My bedroom."

"It'll all fix." Spencer didn't bother to turn around as he passed a wall that hadn't been completely mangled. "Maybe I put it in the kid's room. What was that before? A study? A storage? Something like that?"

"You can't do this to his room, Spencer. He can't see this."

"Unless you have a couple hundred grand to exchange," the man from the stairs explained, "yeah, we're gonna."

Tears burned in her eyes. "You're animals."

"It's business, Teagan. Calm down."

"Then your business stinks." She shook, tears brimming on her bottom eyelashes. "You can't destroy my house because this jackass thinks there are diamonds in the wall."

As if she'd said a code word, the three men crossed their arms, and Spencer rolled his eyes.

She threw her hands in the air, storming down the hall. "What else have you shredded in hopes of finding it?"

She stopped and kicked the bathroom open with her toe.

"Really? *Really!*" The beautiful turquoise wallpaper that she spent weeks searching for then even longer saving for had been sheared into ribbons and dulled by white drywall dust.

"Follow her," someone said. "And keep looking. Not in the boy's room for now."

"Thank goodness for minor miracles." Teagan slammed

the door. "Will, the bathroom is off limits."

"Okay, Mom."

"Stay where it's safe and don't come out." Maybe she was off limits too because she was getting ready to have a nervous breakdown.

"I'm going downstairs. Who wants to help me destroy that?" Teagan shouted then cringed. "Just kidding, Will. Everything's fine."

Heavy boots clomped behind her. "*Don't* follow me too close. I'm up to here—"

"Look, lady, this ain't our ideal, either."

She stopped on the stairs and screamed, "So get out!"

The man genuinely seemed as if he appreciated the level of pissed off she'd reached. "Will do. Soon as we get what we came for."

Teagan's head dropped. Her awful ex had struck again. "And what if you don't? What if he's wrong or he's lying or... what if he's still the same conniving SOB who tricked me into marrying him, and there's nothing more?" Tears slipped down her cheeks, and she couldn't tell why. Was she angry? Or hurt? Was she heartbroken for Will? Or exhausted? Violated?

"It won't be pretty." He shook his head slightly. "Let's only cross that bridge if we come to it."

Teagan pinched the bridge of her nose. "I hate you, Spencer Shaw!"

Then, depleted, she went downstairs to watch as they destroyed her house for blood diamonds. She hoped that maybe they could find them without ripping the rest of her house apart—or maybe she'd get to her purse and call 9-1-1.

CHAPTER THIRTY-TWO

NOAH'S HEAD SWAM from the time at the graveyard, and he still had to shake the cobwebs from the quiet time he'd spent with Lainey. He sat at his home office desk and tried to make heads and tails of purchase orders for parts, but all he saw was numbers that blurred together. Maybe he needed to go kick back in front of the television or see if Bella wanted to play football.

As of yet, she'd not been convinced of its merits, but he was wearing her down. She was addicted to a word scramble game on his phone, and while he knew he shouldn't let her play on it all the time, it helped him get a few minutes in on these purchase orders.

The purchase orders weren't working today. Neither was he, so she was done with phone time. "Ladybug, where you at?"

"Right here," she said a split second later, and Noah jumped back.

"Hey, I didn't know you were right there."

"I have a problem," she whispered.

He patted his knee. "Hop on."

Bella crawled onto his lap and laid her head against his chest. "Mommy always said if I did something wrong, I was supposed to tell her."

"Did you do something wrong?"

She propped up. "I'm not sure."

"Try me, and I can help you figure it out."

"I know I'm not supposed to eavesdrop, right?" she asked hesitantly.

His stomach tightened, wondering what she might have heard. "Right. Did you hear something you maybe shouldn't have?"

"I think so."

Well, hell. "Recently?"

She nodded.

Ugh. This wasn't what he wanted to talk about. "With Teagan?"

Bella nodded again.

"Okay." Noah ran his hand into his hair, for the first time appreciating that it had gotten long enough that he could tear it out. Had Bella heard him in bed with Teagan? "So…"

Nothing came to him. He didn't want to say too much, or not enough. Maybe he should call Teagan and ask what do. He hadn't gone anywhere near that section of the parenting blogs because he figured he had *years*. Or maybe not.

"When two people love each other…" Noah pinched the bridge of his nose, positive that he was going to break into hives.

"I know you love her," Bella interrupted. "But she sounded like she was screaming."

His face flamed. "Yeah." Noah inhaled and sent up a prayer for strength. "About that. When two people think something is… *fun*—"

Bella's face pinched. "Maybe you should eavesdrop. I'm not sure that we're communicating."

His eyebrow crooked. "I'm sorry?"

"Will FaceTimed you, and I answered. *I'm sorry*. But we

eavesdropped. And Teagan is shouting."

Noah's brow furrowed. "Now?"

She nodded.

Unease hyperfocused his attention. "Where's the phone, bug?"

Bella scurried into the hall and came back in with his cell phone wrapped in a pink blanket, tucked into a baby carrier. Noah grabbed it, searching Will's bored face. "Hey, buddy."

"Hi, Noah!"

"What's going on?" He kept his voice calm even as his heartbeat jackhammered.

"These guys are here, and I'm not allowed to leave my room." He leaned close to the phone, his eyes big, as if he was surprised and concerned. "And Mom is shouting."

"At who—"

"The battery is about to die—"

FaceTime showed the call ended, and panic like Noah had never known seized him. "Come on, Bella. Let's go."

CHAPTER THIRTY-THREE

A T THE BOTTOM of the stairs, Noah lifted Bella as he had when she was a toddler and put her on his hip. He bolted across their yard and hopped the small fence to the closest neighbor, the 9-1-1-calling Mrs. Eller, and rang the doorbell. No answer.

Noah growled under his breath. She was home. Her car was there, and he'd spied her peeking out her window several times that day. Noah banged on the door twice. Come on, come on. "Mrs. Eller."

Finally he heard the shuffle of footsteps on the other side and the click of a dead bolt unlocking. Such simple sounds made his insides celebrate as her door inched open and a middle-aged woman peered out.

No doubt, he was intimidating to look at, especially when he knew that she'd called 9-1-1 on him for burning dinner and started the Eagle's Ridge grapevine extravaganza on his first day back in town.

"Hello, Mrs. Eller," Bella said with more manners than Noah could muster.

Mrs. Eller inched the door wider with a somewhat embarrassed face.

Maybe one day they would have a discussion about not calling 9-1-1 on neighbors when it wasn't needed. But that wasn't today. "I need you to watch Bella. It's important."

"An *emergency*," Bella added.

Noah cringed, not wanting this lady to involve the authorities before he figured out what was going on.

Suddenly more interested, Mrs. Eller shot an interested look at Noah. "Really?"

"Hang tight on this one. Please. You can call the cops if you don't hear back from me in thirty minutes."

"Why thirty minutes if it's an emergency now?"

"Because I don't know that it's an emergency now."

"I do," Bella shared.

Noah gritted his teeth but put on his most earnest, trustworthy face. "I'd like to check it out first."

"Hmm."

"Do you have Teagan Shaw's phone number?" Because everyone seemed to have Teagan's phone number for their crisis du jour.

"Well, yes," the woman mumbled.

"Lainey told me I could trust you. That if I ever needed a trusted, helping hand, you could be a go-to." He gave her an earnest look. "Thirty minutes. If you can't get ahold of Teagan, call the cops."

"Okay," she agreed, taking Bella by the hand and inside.

With Bella safely deposited with the person who would call for help at likely the twenty-nine-minute mark, Noah sprinted back toward his house, jumped over the fence, and rushed inside.

He moved toward his gun safe and loaded up. By the time his keys hit the ignition in his truck, he was able to take on a small enemy unit. He had a Glock tucked in his waistband for easy access and a shotgun resting on the passenger seat.

He drove safe, but he hauled ass, skipping every light and sign that told him to slow down or stop. When Noah hit

Teagan's street, he parked two houses away.

Noah passed the front door, stepped into the bushes, and crept against the cedar plank wall. He peeked inside a window and saw nothing then dropped to a crouch before hustling around the side of her home.

Safely out of view of windows and the street, he stood and moved toward the backyard, pausing long enough to see a fresh pile of cigarette butts. But this time, there were white ones mixed with brown-tipped butts too.

Two people he didn't know were prowling around, likely inside.

He angled for a look into another window, seeing the living room—and two men with Teagan. Her head faced the floor as though she were distraught, but her fists were balled into a tight, angry knot.

One man was twice the width of the other, and the slighter one stood to her side talking. The larger man lifted his arms and smashed into the wall.

What the…

Noah didn't know if it was a hatchet or a large knife, but they ripped a gaping hole then sliced down. *Like her insulated shed.*

Teagan's hallways were made of cedar plank with some accent areas covered in decorative stone. But her upstairs and downstairs living spaces were framed only by the wood.

The man in front of the wall methodically tore apart her drywall. What were they looking for?

The man next to her put an arm on her shoulder, patting her as though to offer comfort, and Noah saw red—until Teagan backed up and swung.

His pulse froze. As much as he wanted to holler hell yeah, there was no telling who they were or how they would react.

But neither man flinched.

Noah crept toward the back door and found the white cigarette butts again. But they had been stubbed out a different way. He dropped to his knees and stared. Shit, three people?

Was that her ex-husband? The man who'd tried to touch her? The one who went on expeditions and wouldn't let her sell the house without telling him, who wanted to stop by a few weeks ago but didn't care about seeing his own child…

Her ex-husband wasn't a treasure hunter. He sounded more like a drug runner who was searching for an old stash.

Now this was a different game entirely. Noah wasn't going in ground floor; he was going in from the top down to see what was going on.

Stealthily, he crept back and surveyed the best way to get to the second floor. Not many options. A gutter and the latticework were the best chance he had, but they wouldn't be able to hold his weight for long. He had to move fast. If a neighbor saw him and called the cops, this could go wrong in a split second if those were drug runners.

How to do this? As long as he used the stonework and the wood planking, he could reach Teagan's bedroom with his arm span. Hopefully.

Noah paced back then sprinted toward the house. He rocketed up with one powerful step, hooking his hand on the blue-faded copper drainpipe. He threw his weight toward the edge of the cedar windowsill, and his left hand caught the edge by the tips of his fingers.

Ugh. Noah stretched, breathing hard, and growled as he dropped his right arm, sliding roughly against the exterior wood. His back was against the wall.

"Not my best." Noah grunted, twisting his body until he faced the house.

He took a breath and pressed up to his elbows. Quickly he looked into the room, ducked down, then lofted up again. No one was visible. Noah tore through the window screen, tossed it behind him, then took another deep breath.

The wood edge strained his forearms as sweat beaded at his neckline. He lifted up again, praying that Teagan had left her windows unlatched. No dice. And he had to wait.

Noah listened. Nothing but silence.

Those men were here for a reason. They had stripped her shed and, from the quick glance inside her bedroom, had done the same thing upstairs. They were working their way downstairs. Sooner or later, they'd start ripping the place up again. All Noah needed was patience and for the wood edge to remain in place.

Another round of banging began. Noah catapulted on one arm, slammed his elbow into the window by the lock, then ducked his hand through before unlatching it.

With quick maneuvers, he pushed the window up and dragged himself through, ducking and rolling. Noah landed in a defensive position on the side of her bed with his weapon drawn and eyes on the swivel.

He saw nobody. He heard no one.

He blew out, sweat dripping down his back, then cleared the master bedroom. Then the next room and the next. The bathroom was empty, and he prayed Will's room was not destroyed like this. All he wanted to find was a happy, bored little boy in a perfectly intact room.

Noah rounded the corner, but Will's room was empty. The walls were fine, but the boy was gone.

His heart sank. Footsteps coming up the stairs was the new problem. He pressed against the wall and waited. Two men, different from the ones he saw downstairs, ambled by.

Noah lunged, grabbing the first around his neck and swinging with his ankle to take the stranger to the ground.

The second man attacked, only to meet Noah's elbow. It was a direct strike to his temple, followed by a smart strike to a pressure point in his neck.

Stunned, both men lay on the ground as the first man attempted to push up. Noah tazed him and pressed his fingers into the second man's carotid artery. *Five, four, three, two, one. Out.* That man went limp as the first man twitched.

He searched them for their weapons. Keeping an eye out for other threats, he bound their hands and feet with plastic zip ties. A quick perusal of Teagan's linen closet revealed cloth napkins, and Noah fashioned gags for both men.

A moment later, the one he had choked out was tied to the bathroom sink and the toilet, and the other man was tied to a four-inch pipe that ran through Teagan's walk-in closet.

"Will?" he whispered.

No sign of the kid, and Noah headed downstairs, creeping for the living room.

He had seen a lot of hell over the years, but it had never been personal. Teagan was sitting in the middle of her couch with her head buried in her hands, surrounded by the stuffing from her couch. That was a hard thing to take.

She looked up, and Noah's despair turned to hope. He pressed his finger to his lips, and she gave an almost imperceptible nod.

The two men near her were in an intense argument. Noah's job got much easier. He crept close, passing Teagan and motioning for her to run out then breathing easier when she did.

Noah's right fist flew, slamming into the base of the smaller man's skull. He collapsed with one punch.

The other man lunged for his wall hatchet, but Noah was fast on the draw. The barrel of the Glock rested against the man's temple before he could reach.

"Your buddy's knocked out. The two men upstairs, immobilized. And you have the business end of my service weapon pointed against your head, asshole. You shouldn't have messed with my girl."

"I'm just the muscle, buddy. You know how this goes. Don't do anything stupid." Then his muscles jerked.

Noah didn't care about protocol or what he should do with his weapon. He didn't want a dead body hanging over Teagan's head and scaring Will when he could immobilize the man without taking his life. Instead he drilled the floor plate of his Glock into the man's temple.

"Another one bites the dust," Noah mumbled, dropping him. "Teagan, there were four of them?"

"Yes." She peeked around the corner.

"Got 'em, then." Noah secured the downed men as he saw the first police car pull up outside the front window. He guessed he had taken more than thirty minutes. "Where's Will?"

Teagan's face fell. "What do you mean, *where's Will*? Where is Will?"

She spun in a circle then raced upstairs.

That wasn't what he needed. He had people tied upstairs. Noah raced after Teagan, needing to calm her down and look for her son.

Maybe Will had slipped out to look for help. They needed to check a neighbor's. At the top of the stairs, he found Teagan close to hyperventilating as she walked room to room with wide eyes, opening closet doors.

Noah wrapped Teagan against him. "He's fine. Nobody

hurt you. They didn't touch him. He's a smart kid."

"Then where is he?" she cried as tears streamed down her face. "Will? Will!"

"He slipped out the door. He called the cops." Noah eased Teagan down the stairs and opened the front door, then he motioned for a police officer to get out of the car as another squad car pulled up.

For all he knew this was the entire Eagle's Ridge force, and they would have no idea what to do with this crime scene or with the mother whose son was missing.

The next two minutes were filled with questions that erased the possibility that Will had called them and was at a neighbor's. Noah couldn't imagine how Teagan felt. Her tears never stopped.

Four men were arrested, led out of the house, and Teagan refused to look at her ex-husband as he offered a halfhearted apology on the way out the door.

Time seemed at a standstill. Noah didn't know what to do—

"*No!* I'm not leaving. Are you out of your mind?" Teagan snarled at the newest detective to enter her house.

He'd been advised to give them space since he was part of their investigation, but now his woman was attacked. He came closer and put his arm around her. He kissed the top of her head, giving her as much comfort as he could with a squeeze. Not that it would do a lot of good.

"They want me to go to the police station. I'm not leaving."

"If she's not ready, she's not ready," Noah said.

The detective and Teagan argued, and Teagan didn't need Noah to stick up for her. Noah paced the length of the foyer.

Where would he have gone? He pinched the bridge of his

nose—and froze.

A cold shiver of hope slid over his shoulders, and Noah crouched down, running his fingers along the baseboard.

Click.

The hiding place under the staircase, the coolest place Bella had ever seen, clicked as a secret panel opened. Noah got on his hands and knees and crawled into the small, dark space under the staircase. He scooted over darkened flashlights and dolls, blocks and books, until he reached the farthest corner where the stairs met the first floor. Ducked and wrapped into a little ball was a very scared five-year-old who hid in his secret spot where he believed no one could ever find him.

"Noah?" Will asked quietly.

The only light in the crawlspace was that flooding the room from the now-open secret door. Will had locked himself in and hadn't turned on the flashlight.

Noah put a hand on his back, and Will shook. "It's me, and everything is fine."

"Are you sure?" he finally whispered.

"Yeah, buddy, I'm sure. Your mom's in the hall. The police are here, and everything is fine."

Quick as a flash of lightning, Will launched into Noah's arms and curled himself around his chest, pressing his wet cheeks and T-shirt close, shivering despite the heat. "Mom said stay where it's safe and don't come out."

Noah rubbed Will's back. "It's safe now. Everything's okay. I've got you now."

"Thank you." Will sniffed. "For saving me."

Oh, kid. He eased to where there was more room and pulled Will into his lap to hug him. "I think you have it backward, little man. If you hadn't told Bella what was going on, I couldn't have come help. *I* need to thank *you*."

"I couldn't wait any longer." Teagan crawled into the space under the stairs. "I'm coming in."

"The more the merrier." Will wasn't ready to move yet, and this was where he needed to be.

Will clung tight. "I love you, Noah."

Definitely where he needed to be. "I love you too, kid."

CHAPTER THIRTY-FOUR

T HE TABLE WAS decorated with Bella and Will's handmade Thanksgiving Day crafts. Multicolored marshmallows topped the sweet potato casserole, and the broccolini served as the focal point of conversation with the kids. Skinny broccoli. Tree broccoli. Pencil broccoli. They'd renamed broccolini. This was the first Thanksgiving where Noah had found himself at the head of the table and staring at his future.

Almost.

"It's perfect!" Teagan lifted the golden turkey off his counter and groaned as she shuffled to the table. "And heavy!"

He jumped up, pushed the chair back, and stepped to her. Swiftly he lessened her load and transferred the platter to the table. "You outdid yourself." He took her hand and hugged her toward his chest. "Thank you."

He gave her a quick squeeze and a kiss on the back of her head that made Will and Bella giggle, then Teagan sat at the far end of the table.

Now, this was his future.

They settled at the table, and Teagan smiled. "Before we dig in, should we tell them?"

Noah leaned back as though considering. "I don't know. I think we should torture them until dessert."

"No! No! No!" Bella and Will cried.

He laughed. "Well, as happy as I am to have Teagan and

Will staying with us while their house is fixed, we decided to ask the both of you to help us find a house that is *ours*."

Teagan beamed. "One that we're going to pick out together."

"The four of us?" Bella squealed.

"Yes," Noah answered. "We're not in a rush—"

Bella clapped. "Let's pick one out tonight!"

So much for thinking Bella held on to nostalgic notions of where she grew up with her mother. But as Teagan had pointed out, Bella had Lainey firmly in her heart, and the kid wasn't much attached to the house. Unless they took the fairy gardens into consideration, and those could come with. Still, Noah was worried. "And, ladybug."

"Yes?" She beamed.

"I want to make sure you're comfortable with this."

"Why wouldn't I be?"

He tilted his head. "Because this is where you lived with your mom."

Bella tilted her head, thinking over his sentiments. "She's not in the house. She's at the graveyard."

The kid tugged at his heartstrings, every day.

"And she's an angel. So even if she was here, she'd just move."

Will nodded. "Bella was her angel. That's what she called her."

Noah glanced at Teagan, and her eyes were watery. "That's true, baby."

"You were her angel," Will told Bella. "And now she's yours."

Bella nodded as though Will had just brought both adults' hearts to a standstill. Noah's heart was full. "Happy Thanksgiving, family. I love you."

★　★　★

THE PILLOWS WERE stacked underneath the dining room table, and Bella leaned against Will as they piled another blanket in front of them.

"We did it, ya know?" Bella moved two of her dolls closer, knocking over one of his ninja warriors.

Will grabbed the ninja warrior and rearranged the dolls to hold it up. "Like this. So they all sit up."

She elbowed him. "Did you even hear what I said?"

"I heard you. That we did it." He elbowed back. "What did we do?"

Bella rolled her eyes and groaned, taking one of her dolls back and moving her to the other side. The other doll and the ninja warrior both toppled.

"That wasn't very nice." Will took both and shoved them under a pillow.

"Neither was that." She snapped her doll into her arms. "Your mom and Uncle Noah. *We did that.*"

Will stopped and turned. "Oh, I know. We said we would. And we did."

She clapped around the doll in her arms. "Now we get to be best friends like Uncle Noah and my mom were."

Will banged his ninja warrior against the doll in his hand. "*I know.*"

"Do you think that we should tell them?" She asked, suddenly worried that they might get in trouble. Though her uncle Noah seemed very happy and Teagan too.

"I don't know." He let the toys rest in his lap.

"Let's go see them."

"They're in here." Will crawled underneath the table, and Bella followed.

They stayed on their hands and knees, crawling through the dining room then the kitchen until they came into the living room. The TV blasted football. No one talked.

"Shhh," Will hushed for no reason.

"I know!"

"Shhh!"

They crept to the side of the couch where four grown-up feet dangled over the edge.

Will pivoted on the back of his heels into a crouch. "Shhh."

"*I know!*" Then Bella sealed her lips and used her fingers to zip them.

Convinced she wouldn't make any noise, he commenced the creeping, and they worked their way around the front of the couch, where Teagan lay next to her uncle Noah. Neither looked at the TV.

Snore.

They jumped. Then laughed. Both slapped their hands over their mouths to stop the giggles as, wide-eyed, they stared at Uncle Noah snoring again.

"Hurry," Will whispered, and they scurried on hands and knees to the other side of the room.

With their backs flat against the wall, waving each other enough secret hand signals to decide they were far enough away, they gave thumbs-ups, giving the okay to talk.

"Noah snores very loud," Will said. "Like a jackhammer."

"Maybe we wished on too many dandelions."

He nodded. "Or that shooting star."

Bella shook her head. "That wasn't a shooting star. It was an airplane. I know things."

They crept around the corner, staring at her uncle Noah, snoring *like a jackhammer,* and Teagan, who maybe had lost some of her hearing. Otherwise, she would have awakened.

"Maybe it wasn't an airplane."

"Told you. Shooting star." Will stuck his chin up. "*I know things.*"

A real shooting star. Wow.

"What do you think's gonna happen when Santa shows up?" Will asked.

Bella squealed quietly, and Will toppled on top of her, sealing his hands over her mouth.

Finally, he pulled back. "You have to be quiet."

"Why? If a shooting star got me you for a brother, think about what Santa's gonna bring! A whole fairy tale."

FORD

7 BRIDES FOR 7 SOLDIERS
BOOK 7

SAMANTHA CHASE

ABOUT FORD

There are three things Ford Garrison wants more than anything: to build, to report to no one, and the chance to live his life without the prying eyes of the good folks of Eagle's Ridge. Having spent ten years in the Navy as part of their construction battalion, he was able to live out most of that dream. Two out three wasn't bad, right? Now that he's out of the service, things aren't falling into place quite as easily as he hoped and he ends up back home with all eyes on him.

It wasn't as if Callie had gone out of her way to end up in Ford's path, but somehow that happened all on its own and the town gossips were having a field day! Could she help it that she was living in the house Ford had hoped to claim as his own or that the work on his grandmother's ranch meant they were living not fifty-feet away from each other?

Ford was determined to come home, do a job to help his grandmother and leave. Callie James is a distraction and she represents everything he has spent years running away from. Now he's at odds with his friends, his family and himself about where his home and future are going to be.

Could he walk away from Eagle's Ridge a second time?

ABOUT THE AUTHOR

CRISTIN HARBER is a *New York Times* and *USA Today* bestselling romance author. She writes sexy romantic suspense, military romance, new adult, and contemporary romance. Readers voted her onto Amazon's Top Picks for Debut Romance Authors in 2013, and her debut Titan series was both a #1 romantic suspense and #1 military romance bestseller.

Connect with Cristin by email at Cristin@CristinHarber.com and join her newsletter! Text TITAN to 66866 for exclusive emails.

The Titan Series:
Book 1: Winters Heat
Book 1.5: Sweet Girl
Book 2: Garrison's Creed
Book 3: Westin's Chase
Book 4: Gambled
Book 5: Chased
Book 6: Savage Secrets
Book 7: Hart Attack
Book 7.5: Sweet One
Book 8: Black Dawn
Book 8.5: Live Wire
Book 9: Bishop's Queen
Book 10: Locke and Key
Book 11: Jax

The Delta Series:

Book 1: Delta: Retribution
Book 2: Delta: Rescue*
Book 3: Delta: Revenge
Book 4: Delta: Redemption
Book 5: Delta: Ricochet

*The Delta Novella in Liliana Hart's MacKenzie Family Collection

The Only Series:

Book 1: Only for Him
Book 2: Only for Her
Book 3: Only for Us
Book 4: Only Forever

7 Brides for 7 Soldiers:

Ryder (#1) – Barbara Freethy
Adam (#2) – Roxanne St. Claire
Zane (#3) – Christie Ridgway
Wyatt (#4) – Lynn Raye Harris
Jack (#5) – Julia London
Noah (#6) – Cristin Harber
Ford (#7) – Samantha Chase

Each Titan, Delta, and 7 Brides book can be read as a standalone (except for Sweet Girl), but readers will likely best enjoy the series in order. The Only series must be read in order.

ACKNOWLEDGEMENTS

There is an unsung hero that I'll never meet again, and I can't help but be inspired by you. One day soon, I'll get to tell your tale, but until then, please know that on a magical day in Disney World, you made a dream come true for a little prince and princess. Thank you from the bottom of my heart. You reaffirmed my faith in true heroes and chivalry, and that's a lot to take on at your young age. My only regret is that we didn't take a picture and hug, but at the time, I wasn't aware of how deep an impact you made on me. I'm forever grateful for your kindness.

Thank you to my readers—new ones who have found me through this project, and Team Titan, who stay by my side through every project I try. My muse is a wild one. I listen to where my heart takes me, despite the wave of trends, and since the first day we met, through every series and happily ever after, we remain consistent. I give to you as much as you give back, and as I pen my acknowledgments before Thanksgiving, I know that my readers are why I have so much to be thankful for. *wipes away tears*

Many thanks to Barbara Freethy for the fantastic opportunity to work on this project, and more importantly, with you. Barbara was on the first self-publishing panel I'd attended. Watching what she had to say quite possibly changed the trajectory of my career, so this is a very full circle moment. I'm honored to write alongside her in the 7 Brides for 7 Soldiers series along with the incredibly talented Roxanne St. Claire,

Christie Ridgway, Lynn Raye Harris, Julia London, and Samantha Chase.

A massive shout out to the team that worked on NOAH. This list doesn't begin to do justice, but thank you to Angela McRae from Red Adept for the stellar editing, Patricia Patti for your eagle eyes, Judie Bouldry for always being on top of everything, Danielle Sanchez, Tara Gonzalez, and Amber Noffke of InkSlinger PR for your hard work, Jenn Wood for her fantastic opinions on Noah, Trish Kluge for thinking for me when I didn't have time for one more to-do, and Damonza for the beautiful book cover design.

And finally, in my most extended acknowledgments section ever, thank you to my family for teaching and reminding me to be Titan Strong. xoxo

Made in the USA
Lexington, KY
04 December 2017